A full list of Vivian's print titles is available on her website

www.vivianarend.com

PRAISE FOR VIVIAN AREND

"Vivian Arend does a wonderful job of building the atmosphere and the other characters in this story so that readers will be sucked into the world and looking forward to the rest of the books in the series."
~ *Library Journal*

"Steamy and sweet complete with a whole host of colourful side characters and enough sub-plots to get your teeth into. A fab read!"
~ *Scorching Book Reviews*

"There's a real chemistry between the characters, laced with humor and snappy dialogue and no shortage of steamy sex scenes to keep things lively. The result is an entertaining, spicy romance."
~ *Publishers Weekly*

Silver Mine is an outstanding story. The author creates a world that invites readers for the ride of their lives."
~ *Coffee Time Romance Reviews*

Arend offers constant action and thrills, and her characters are so captivating and nuanced that readers will have a hard time guessing who the villains really are.
~ *RT Book Reviews*

LAIRD WOLF

TAKHINI SHIFTERS: BOOK 2

VIVIAN AREND

Laird Wolf
Copyright © 2015 by Arend Publishing Inc.
ISBN: 9781989507896
Edited by Anne Scott
Cover by Croco Designs
Proofed by Sharon Muha

NOTE TO READERS

The *Takhini Shifters* are novellas set in the *Granite Lake* and *Takhini Wolves* world. Some of the heroes and heroines you'll meet will be new, some vaguely familiar from their appearances in previous books, but you don't have to have read the earlier books to enjoy these stand-alone stories.

These are lighthearted, sexy reads meant to take you away for a short while, and to make you smile as the hero and heroine find their happily-ever-after.

Enjoy!

Timeline/story overlap
LAIRD WOLF takes place in June around the start of BLACK GOLD.

Characters in Laird Wolf who have appeared in previous books:
Damon Black: Copper King
Addie MacShay: Copper King (texting only)
Jim and Lillie Halcyon: Copper King

The trails of the world be countless,
and most of the trails be tried;
You tread on the heels of the many,
till you come where the ways divide;
And one lies safe in the sunlight,
and the other is dreary and wan,
Yet you look aslant at the Lone Trail,
and the Lone Trail lures you on.

"The Lone Trail"—Robert Service

1

---

*A*thin spray of water rose behind the wheels of his bike as Damon Black powered down a lonely stretch of Scottish highway and considered all possible meanings of the phrase *one hell of a ride.*

The second wave of the storm rumbled louder than the pathetic engine under him, thunderclouds roiling overhead like some National Geographic feature played at high speed. As he closed in on the imposing Sterling-Wylde Manor, it looked as if his shitty luck was going to continue.

His last-minute flight from New York to Inverness had turned into a redeye after being delayed on the tarmac for six hours, putting him into the Scottish airport at five a.m. The classic custom bike he'd booked wasn't there for some reason, and he'd snatched up the only thing they had on the lot. The best Damon could say about his mode of transportation was it had two wheels and an engine not powered by hamsters.

Still, with a sense of urgency driving him, instead of wasting time, he'd headed into the middle of nowhere on his rescue mission. The first rain shower had gotten him wet, but the highway had been well maintained, and he'd pushed on. Now with the sky turning cobalt and shots of silver reflecting off the surface of the distant lake, Damon figured he was about to be completely drenched.

June in Scotland. Lovely.

The road was no longer smooth, and he swerved to avoid massive potholes, his teeth chattering as his entire body vibrated. Mud lifted off the bumpy asphalt, sticking to him as the wind blew in violently from the north. Only the heat of his shifter body kept him from going into hypothermia.

He put his head down and ignored the rolling Scottish landscape, which under better circumstances might have registered as pretty. All he wanted was to get to his destination and make sure Addie MacShay was safe.

This is what friendship meant. It meant he was headed into the middle of bloody nowhere in northern Scotland to rescue the best friend of his best friend's wife. He'd never met the woman, but here he was, jetlagged and hungry, and if he wasn't mistaken, three seconds away from swimming in his clothes.

Damon curled up tighter behind the handlebars and increased his speed to maximum, screaming around the sharp curves leading toward what was admittedly an impressive estate. Whatever had brought Addie to this godforsaken place, the people had money.

He adjusted his mindset a few moments later as he passed through the gated entranceway. One side of the massive rock wall held its twisted iron gate in position, albeit rusted and worn, but the other side lay toppled in the grass. An octopus of bent metal reached skyward.

The faint drizzle increased in volume, and Damon

cursed harder. He was going to show up looking like a vagabond no matter what he did.

As if trying to increase his level of misery, the back tire on his lame beast of a bike chose that instant to blow, sending the motorcycle skidding from under him. He bounced over the cracked asphalt and onto the grass, momentum propelling him like a rock from a slingshot as he rolled out of control over the torn-up lawn.

He landed in an inglorious heap, waist deep in a sludge-bottomed fishpond.

Damon sat there for a moment, rain pouring down on his head, his helmet tossed aside to let the fresh water wash away some of the duckweed. Strands of hair stuck to his face, and everything from his pants to his boots were filled with water.

His wolf was not amused.

He chuckled. Yup, this trip had been one hell of a ride so far, and he'd barely started.

No luggage—it had decided to go somewhere in India instead of Inverness. According to his research, there was limited if any phone service in the area, which meant if he was in the wrong place it would be hell to get directions, and now here he sat.

At least his day couldn't get any more fucked up.

Motion from the front door of the enormous edifice pulled his attention to the building towering over him. He couldn't fault the architecture—his best friend Jim would love to see it. The massive stone bricks that made up the entrance of the keep gave it an old-world flair while the vines curling around masonry softened the imposing castle-like structure.

He hoped to God it had modern plumbing.

Damon dragged himself from the pond and sloshed

back to his bike, hauling the broken beast to vertical and manhandling it down the road to the base of the wide staircase.

He kicked the stand into position then turned, glancing up the stairs to discover two men in their late fifties watching him. One might've stepped out of the pages of a Harry Potter book, his long, crimson robes enveloping a thin body. A thin, pointy nose was barely visible from under the cowl covering his head, but even from a distance Damon sensed his disapproval.

"You can't put that pile of trash there." The second man spoke, a distinctively feline lilt to his smooth voice. He stepped into the light and gave Damon a clear shot of groomed masculine perfection.

Huh. *Yawn.*

GQ dressers didn't impress him much, but Damon supposed the other man might turn a few female heads, at least if they were into the crisp, tailored-suit thing. But he'd look more in place in a New York office tower, or in the Inverness business sector, than here in the highlands.

The dude gave Damon a perfunctory glance before sniffing, pulling a handkerchief from the pocket of his immaculate suit jacket and dabbing it against his mouth. "This is a private residence. You'll have to leave. Now."

Damon's wolf bared its teeth, ready and willing for them to deal with the situation in a more physically satisfying and bloody manner. The human side fought for dominance, not letting the internal battle he was waging show.

Damn, hot-tempered wolf. Everything that was wrong about the day would flare to nuclear-meltdown levels if he let the beast have its way. He had to turn this around before things got out of control. Damon clenched his fists and attempted diplomacy. "I—"

The suit waved a hand in dismissal, turning as if to leave. "Get out of here."

It wasn't the best time to poke at Damon, or Damon's wolf. He slammed the beast down before snapping a response. "I know this is a private residence. I'm here for Addie."

Both men blinked, the professor-type shifting uneasily from side to side as Damon made his way up the stairs to the landing. "She didn't tell us anyone was coming to visit."

"Is it a problem? Her having visitors?" Damon didn't bother to keep the growl out of his question. He understood their hesitation. He looked like a tramp, but expecting anyone in his condition to just get the hell out without offering help hadn't made a good first impression.

The fact his wolf really wanted to chase them both made it difficult to stay attentive. Damon forced his animal side under control as he wondered what kind of shifters he was dealing with. He couldn't pinpoint their scent, other than definitely feline.

The asshole in the suit came to a decision. He made a movement as if he was about to offer his hand in greeting before noticing the weeds and muck clinging to Damon and casually tucking his hands into his pockets. "I'm Alastair, and this is my brother Niall. We're the owners of Sterling-Wylde Manor."

"*One* of us is the owner," Niall snapped as he stepped forward, his fingers linked together as he stared down the bridge of his nose at Damon before offering a sniff of his own. His lips twisted, but he nodded. "I'll summon Addie for you."

Summon?

"Tell her Damon is here."

Damon folded his arms over his chest, taking a defensive stance against one of the columns supporting the grand entranceway they stood under. He wasn't sure the message had gotten through that he was coming. He hoped she didn't screw things up and deny knowing any Damon.

Niall paused next to an ancient intercom system mounted beside the imposing dual-front doors and poked at the buttons. His *summons* sent, Niall glowered from beside the door, while Alastair stood just out of arm's reach and stared unblinkingly.

Damon ignored them. Instead, he removed his leather jacket and T-shirt then used the soaking fabric to wipe away the mud and weeds clinging to his face and arms.

Damn cats. Self-righteous, egotistical and no damn sense of humour. Then again, his wolf was pacing back and forth under his skin like a rabid animal that longed to sink its teeth into someone.

Damon twisted the shirt in his hands, wringing out the water. He returned Alastair's stare as he rotated his hands slowly, a feral smile curling his lips as he refused to break eye contact.

He figured they were about three seconds away from Alastair peeing his expensive pants right there on the marble landing when the door to the side of Niall creaked open and a small woman stepped out.

He'd seen pictures of her, but they paled in comparison to the real thing. Her dark brown hair was pulled back in a neat braid, her skin a smooth, creamy bronze. High cheekbones sat below a pair of whisky-coloured eyes Damon desperately wanted to peer into more closely. He'd also like to examine in great detail her perfect red lips that were pulling into an O of surprise.

She barely came up to the middle of his chest, but he figured that would be okay. He'd be able to lift her, probably with one arm. Heck, if he got her into the right position? With a sturdy wall behind her, and the legs currently peeking out below the edge of the pristine pencil skirt wrapped around his hips...

Damon's wolf was at high alert and ready to pounce, and for once in his life the man agreed one hundred percent with the animal. *Everything* about Addie made him hard.

She'd been checking him over as well in the brief moment it'd taken to fall in lust. Her gaze darted over his messy hair before traveling down his naked chest and landing firmly on the growing erection behind his jeans. Her throat moved in a hard swallow as her eyes widened, then before he could say a word, she rushed across the distance and threw herself into his arms.

ADDIE HAD BEEN LAYING personal bets how her best friend would come to her rescue. Considering Lillie had married a billionaire, some of those scenarios had involved *Skyfall*-worthy helicopter chases, where men in camouflage gear swarmed the Sterling-Wylde estate and pulled her to safety. Or a more romantic fantasy, where a mysterious, dark stranger would slip in unannounced one night, sneak up to her bedroom in the tower, and after proving he was worthy of her trust, become her shadowy protector as she went through her daily tasks.

Never in a million years could even her fertile imagination have dreamt up a soaking-wet beggar with sky-blue eyes and a body built for sin. But if this was what she got?

Holy moly, she'd take him.

Which was why she'd gone on the attack, clutching his neck as she curled herself around him like a twist tie. He opened his mouth, probably to protest, so she did the only thing she could think of before he blew it and said something that messed up her skimpy plans.

She kissed him. Hard. Locking their lips together as she used her full strength to tighten her legs around his hips and keep him close.

She braced herself for the impact of physical contact. With her unique talents—*thank you so very much, Mom and Dad*—getting close to someone always had repercussions. She refused to focus on what might happen, utterly aware that the Sterling-Wylde boys were watching in slack-jawed astonishment. So she concentrated on Damon and making a convincing job of the kiss. Everything would fall apart if he didn't go along with her charade.

Two seconds later she wasn't worried about him giving them away. Instead she was captivated by his kiss. In the way he'd placed one hand under her hips to hold her close, the other sliding intimately up her back until his fingers were buried in her hair. His lips moved enticingly against hers as his tongue danced past her teeth.

Sensation flooded in as the fuzzy curtain between them began to disappear. She'd surprised him—it had been enough to stop the rush of emotions from overwhelming her, but his excitement and curiosity were slicing through the barrier.

Addie broke off the kiss as quickly as she could, forcing a smile to her lips as she pressed both hands against his chest—*oh my goodness, his naked chest*. She'd seen pictures of Damon while visiting her best friend, but the shots of him with Lillie's husband had all been fully clothed. Now she was up close and personal with rock-solid muscles covered with golden skin, a hint of blond curls dusting his pectorals that she wanted to drag her fingertips through—

It took every bit of willpower possible to push back until he set her feet on the ground and there was air between them. She dragged her hands free and locked her fingers together to stop from petting him again. "Damon. What an awesome surprise."

His lips curled as he offered her a cocky, confident smile. "You should've known I'd visit."

Addie twirled on the spot, glancing between her hosts. "Alastair, Niall, I'd like you to meet Damon Black. My boyfriend."

Three simultaneous noises greeted her, the low chuckle at her back less expected than the rapidly hidden gasps of dismay from the Sterling-Wylde boys.

Damon placed his hands firmly on her shoulders and laughter danced in his voice as he spoke. "That's what I am. Yup. Addie's boyfriend. Nice to meet you both."

"Did you plan on staying, Mr. Black?" Niall intoned, ignoring the pleasantries.

"I'm so sorry." Addie rushed forward, removing Damon's hands from her shoulders and creating a barrier between the cats and the wolf who was bristling with disapproval. "I should've spoken with both of you before, but Damon wasn't sure he would be able to get away, and I didn't think it was worthwhile asking before his trip became certain."

"It's most inconvenient," Alastair protested, his voice rising. "This is a terrible time—"

"It's fine," Niall interrupted, glaring at his brother. "I'm sure Addie will continue to work diligently. There's no reason why she shouldn't have a visitor."

Alastair hissed his disapproval. "Says you."

The boys stepped toward each other, circling to choose places for their catfight. Addie took advantage of their distraction, glancing over her shoulder at Damon before tilting her head toward the door.

He got the message, picking up his things then joining her.

Niall shook his head, his cowl falling back to reveal sandy-coloured hair shot with grey, pulled into a thin ponytail. "Very well, send him on his way, Alastair. Typically cruel of you. Probably catch his death of pneumonia. It'll be on your head."

"He's not going to die."

"*If* you're lucky. I can already see the newspaper. *Another suspicious death at the Manor*, it'll say, and then—"

"I'll just take him to get cleaned up," Addie interrupted. God, the brothers could go on forever when they started arguing, like two little boys, which is what she'd relegated them to in her mind. "Such a terrible storm, I hope nothing in the garden got crushed."

The Sterling-Wylde boys barely glanced at her, eager to get back to their fight. Niall waved a hand dismissively. "Keep him off the expensive carpets."

"Wait. Where's your luggage?" Alastair demanded, whirling on them as if delighted to have found something else out of place.

"Airline lost it." Damon pulled on his leather jacket, covering up the wide expanse of drool-worthy skin. Addie didn't know if she was happy or sad about that.

Alastair hesitated, narrowing his eyes at his brother before turning back with a wide grin and becoming the consummate host. "I'll send someone around with clothing you can borrow," he offered. "Unless you'd prefer to spend your time in wolf form."

Niall made a noise like he was bringing up a hairball. "Not in the house. Anything else, but no dogs in the house."

"Timber wolf," Damon corrected. "Thank you for the clothes. Your hospitality is truly magnificent. I'm humbled by your gallant offer. I shall treat your possessions with the utmost care."

Good grief. Addie grabbed his arm, hauling him through the grand entrance toward her tower.

The instant they were out of sight she freed herself, striding toward the first set of stairs then dashing up them two at a time.

She raced ahead to discourage conversation. Silent at her side, Damon cased the joint as they crossed marble hallways and skipped past enormous side rooms. Addie eyed their surroundings with appreciation. The interior of the grand estate had been modernized enough it was comfortable, if still on the slightly rustic side.

But the history...that's what she loved. The enormous rooms they passed spoke of grand balls and hunting trips with royalty. Both a political and social playground for the upper class during centuries past, the manor had lost only part of its glory.

And now it was the site of yet another battle, luckily one Addie didn't have to fight.

She guided Damon through the labyrinth of passageways to the staircase leading to her bedroom. They were halfway up the spiral before he spoke.

"Do you have some kind of Rapunzel fantasy?"

Addie shivered, tempted by the other fantasies his deep, growly voice instilled in her far too quickly. "It's the only room I found with a working lock."

"And you had a reason to lock yourself in?"

Deadly anger laced his question. She was pretty sure if she answered *yes*, Alastair and Niall would be bleeding within moments.

Addie paused on the landing outside her door, sending as much calm toward Damon as possible. "No reason, but I was uncomfortable. Pull in your claws, wolf."

He smiled, showing his teeth. "Yes, *sweetheart*."

Oh dear. The boyfriend thing.

She'd have to explain, and soon, but first he was still dripping, a trail of water marking their route through the manor. On the other side of the tower, modern plumbing had been installed in the adjoining room. Decadence spread before them like a chrome-and-marble pleasure garden. Another reason she'd picked the location for her own.

She gestured toward the shower. "You must be freezing. Get cleaned up, and I'll find you something to wear until the clothes arrive."

Damon tossed his leather jacket to the side, his bright blue T-shirt abandoned with it. He popped open the top button on his jeans and lowered the zipper. Addie snapped her gaze back to his face when she realized she was watching him strip with far too much fascination.

Getting naked wasn't a problem for most shifters. It came with the territory, along with bonus goodies like disease-free sex and a keen sense of fertility—i.e. no condoms necessary. At their age no strings attached sex was fun, most of the time.

But she wasn't the type to tumble every Big Bad Wolf she met, which was why even though her cheeks were flaming hot, it was definitely time for her to put some space between them.

Too bad that wasn't his agenda.

Nope. He was staring, the deep rumble of his voice trapping her and nailing her feet to one spot. "*Awww, sweetheart, don't go. I could really use your help. You can soap all my hard-to-reach places.*"

His jeans joined the rest of the clothing in the pile. His boots were there too, black with metal straps. There didn't seem to be any underwear, and yes, she was totally examining his clothing to keep from looking at *naked him.*

"I'm not showering with you right now," Addie said as evenly as possible.

Another rumble greeted her—*damn that was sexy*—but thank goodness, the water flicked on.

"*Not now* means *sometime.* I like that idea. Showers are more environmentally friendly when you share. I'm surprised you're not interested in conservation."

"Right. Like you're really environmentally concerned—"

Drat, his distraction had worked. She'd turned to face him and got a full frontal as a reward. For a moment all she could do was flap her jaw. The ripped muscles she'd witnessed all over his upper body weren't alone. They carried on down past the *mumble-mumble in the middle she wasn't ready to let register in her brain* to muscular thighs and calves, and, as he turned, a set of ass cheeks she wanted to dig her teeth into.

"Lordy, your butt is a thing of beauty."

She slammed her mouth closed before she said something specific regarding his other assets.

Damon offered an amused grin over his shoulder. "On that note, I'll stop teasing. I am cold, and I'm hungry too, if that's not being a pain in the ass. I didn't stop for breakfast before I left the airport."

She was a fool, spending time ogling him when she

should have been taking care of him. "As soon as you're dressed, we'll go down for breakfast. It's nearly time."

Damon caught her eye. The power of an alpha wolf stroked her as he offered a confident promise. "It's going to be okay, Addie. I'll take care of you."

She scurried out of the bathroom, a little concerned with how hard the butterflies in her stomach were dancing at his announcement. Her wolf stretched inside, expressing interest in being cared for, and there was no way for Addie to deny it.

His promises, *all* of them, spoken or implied, sounded damn good to her as well.

2

———

*D*amon scrubbed the Scottish scum off his body and from under his nails then hurried to dry off so he could join Addie.

She wasn't what he'd expected, not from what he'd learned over the past months when he'd visited Jim and Lillie. Addie was nothing like his best friend's wife. She was far more independent and bold, and every bit of him was curious to learn more.

Well, every bit except his wolf, which made this an unusual situation. Here they were with a new lady who pushed every *yes* button he had. Normally the animal side of him would be eager to have some fun, especially considering she was a wolf as well. But, nope. After the initial burst of interest, it seemed the other part of him was pouting. Wolfie Damon had withdrawn to someplace deep inside and left him to his humanness.

But considering the love-hate relationship he had with his inner beast, who knew what was wrong? Maybe it was simply pissed about being hauled across the world without enough food.

Addie had retreated to the balcony, the French doors thrown open to let in the morning breeze off the moors. The air was fresh post-storm, and somewhere not too far away a ton of birds were all tweeting their fool heads off.

Damon strolled out to stand next to her, leaning his elbows on the balcony railing as he stared over the landscape. "For the end of the universe this isn't bad, in a muddy, no-fun-in-sight kind of way."

She snorted.

For some reason her response tickled his funny bone. "What? Are you telling me this is downtown Metropolis Scotland?"

The sun shimmered off her smooth brown skin as she twisted toward him, tempting him to take a lick. "From what I heard, anything that isn't five steps off Times Square in New York City is the *back of beyond* to you."

Damon tilted his head, fighting to keep from grinning too hard. "I do have more refined tastes than some."

"In your opinion. Is this what the best-dressed wolves on Wall Street are wearing these days?" She set an unpolished fingernail against the fabric on his hip where he'd wrapped a towel around his groin.

He wasn't sure why he'd covered himself, considering skin was an acceptable alternative. He lowered his voice and invited her wolf to come out and play. "It's more fun to give you something to unwrap."

A burst of laughter escaped, and she poked him in the stomach. "Oh my God, go away."

"Why? Are you telling me we have a platonic relationship? I'm supposed to be your boyfriend."

Addie paused. "About that..."

Damon shook his head. "Hey, no worries, I'm cool with

us being an item. Not sure how we got to this point, but you'll get no arguments from me, *baby*. I'm sure we're damn hot together." He waggled his brows...at her retreating back. She'd twirled on the spot and escaped into the bedroom. "If you keep walking away from me, our conversations are going to take a lot of time."

"Not a conversation if you keep talking nonsense," she admonished over her shoulder. "We've got half an hour to get to the dining hall. You want to know what's going on?"

He sighed dramatically as he settled on the bed, fluffing up the pillows before he piled them against the headboard and leaned back. "Shoot. Tell me what's on your mind, *sweetheart*."

If looks could kill, he would've been eviscerated. This was going to be fun.

"I told you, it's nothing specific, except for constantly being watched."

Damon snickered. "Damn cats."

Addie nodded. "Oh my goodness, *yes*. I mean, I've worked with all kinds of shifters, but these two in particular...?" She visibly shuddered. "I keep expecting to walk into a room and catch Niall grooming himself, and I mean his human form, not his Highland Tiger."

Well, there was a new one. "Highland *Tiger*? Like stripes, and roaring noises, and everything?"

"Their tails are blunt with distinctive black rings, kind of like a raccoon, but yes, tiger markings on their torsos."

"And they make you uncomfortable?" It wasn't really a question. The way she damn near twitched every time she mentioned them was answer enough.

She hesitated then nodded. "I don't like feeling this way about anyone. As if I'm judging them before I know them, but considering they didn't live here a month ago, and they don't *need* to be here, it would be nice to do my job without worrying one or the other is going to walk into whatever room I'm in and spend the next hour silently skulking about."

"What *are* you doing?" Damon asked with sincere curiosity. "This is a strange place for a single woman to traipse to on a job assignment all on her lonesome."

The cutest little frown appeared on her forehead as she sat in the chair in front of the antique makeup table. "You don't know?"

He shook his head. "All I got was the message Lillie wanted me to come and take care of you, so I came."

"*Awwwww.*" Her expression softened. "She's the best."

Damon made a face. "*She's* the best? I'm the one who hauled ass all the way over here to be your watchdog."

Abby gave him a tolerant smile. "Fine. Who's a good boy? You are. You're a very good boy."

"Enough with the dog jokes," he ordered, but he laughed in spite of himself. "Why are we preparing to do battle with the kitty-litter duo?"

"I'm a cataloger. It's my job to break down everything of value now that Lord Sterling-Wylde passed away. The authorities are working on the will." Addie made a face. "Or I should say wills, because four have been found so far—I came across one in the pantry the first week I was here, and another a week later in a bedroom."

The pantry? Something weird was going on.

"But the wills are for the lawyers to mess with. I just need to create the final inventory for when they decide which one of the boys is the actual heir to the manor, Alastair or Niall."

"It's not obvious?"

She snorted. "Ummm, no. Consider this. Lord Sterling-Wylde dies, and two wills are presented—one from Alastair, one from Niall."

"Let me guess. Each names a different heir."

"Bingo. And then I start work and find another version. The boys moved into the manor the next day." She rose to answer a knock on the door.

Suddenly things made more sense. "That's why they're being creepers on you. They both want the place, and think if they're not around it might hurt their chances to inherit."

"Of course that's why they're watching, but it still seems crazy to me. I mean, it's not like them being around can stop me from handing anything I find to the lawyers. Unless the boys plan to do something nefarious, like kill me and hide the body, which seems a little over-the-top dramatic, even for them."

Damon's hackles went up at the thought of anyone laying a finger on her.

She held the door as two uniformed men brought in four ancient suitcases and stacked them on the bench at the foot of the bed. The servants eyed Damon, and he couldn't resist showing his fangs as he smiled.

They hurriedly made their escape.

"Are you planning on being this difficult the entire time you're here?" She stomped across the room to snap open the latches on the first suitcase.

"Hey, I was setting up my disguise. I'm the hot, protective boyfriend who's come to visit you, who you can't keep your hands off." Damon slid off the bed and sauntered to her side, ignoring the retching sounds she was making. "And I'm not difficult at all. I'm low maintenance, really. Feed me, pet me. Meet my physical needs..."

The first suitcase was entirely filled with large pieces of

plaid fabric. Addie grabbed one and thrust it forward. "Sure, love to."

He just about dropped the material. After all her blushing glances, that was the last thing he'd expected to hear. "Really?"

She backed away, disappearing into the bathroom and shouting back at him. "Definitely. There's a leash around here somewhere. I have no problems taking you for walksies a couple of times a day."

Damn, he *liked* her. "You know, you're a wolf as well. All these dog jokes might make people think you don't have any howl in you."

The water turned on, and he strolled closer, hoping for a more revealing glimpse. Nope. Nothing too exciting, unless good oral hygiene was a kink.

She paused in the middle of brushing her teeth to answer him. "That's the trouble with hanging around other shifters. Yes, I'm a wolf, but I spent tons of time with Lillie and her bear parents, and there are a lot of fox shifters here in Scotland." She caught his eye in the mirror before shaking her toothbrush in his direction. "Hurry up. Find something to wear. We leave in five minutes."

And that's how he ended up pacing the halls at her side, an ancient linen shirt covering his upper body and a rather breezy chunk of plaid fastened around his hips. A thorough search of the suitcases hadn't turned up any footwear, so he'd pulled on his boots and was currently ignoring the water squishing between his toes on every step.

"I take it this means you plan on sticking around?" Addie asked as she led him past banners and formal portraits, and what looked to Damon like a museum's worth of artifacts. Plenty of reasons Alastair and Niall would want sole ownership of the manor.

Well, he'd make sure Addie stayed safe. Two pussycats didn't worry him at all. "Of course I'm sticking around. That's why Jim called me."

She guided him down a broad staircase that curled in a clockwise direction. "I'm going to be here for quite a while. I don't want to keep you from your job."

"Nah, don't worry about it. I've got nowhere I need to be."

Damon couldn't resist. Protect Addie—no problem. But there was no reason he couldn't have some fun at the same time. He hopped up on the edge of the railing, the tight-knit wool of his kilt forming the perfect slippery barrier between him and the polished oak. He slid downward rapidly, arms stretched wide to keep his balance, air swirling past as he approached the bottom...

Where an enormous baluster blocked the path between him and main-floor landing.

He had all of three seconds to come up with a solution that didn't end with a pile of broken, tartan-coloured shifter. He timed it perfectly, catching hold of the top wooden knot and letting momentum swing him over the top, landing in a balanced crouch on the antique woven carpet.

A serving girl stood to one side of the Grand Hall, her eyes wide as dinner plates. Damon tipped an imaginary hat in her direction before turning back to the staircase and waiting for Addie.

It didn't take long, and when she hit the lower level she was wearing an angry face.

"Hey, I didn't hurt anything," he protested.

She placed a hand on his back and gave him a shove down the hallway, speaking just loud enough for his wolf ears. "You also flashed poor Charlotte. Did you forget you're not wearing any underwear?"

What kind of question was that? "I'm wearing a kilt."

She didn't seem to think that was enough of an answer. He hurried ahead so he could turn and pace backward, examining her face for clues how to proceed. The haughty expression she was fiercely maintaining was cute enough he was tempted to pick her up and kiss her soundly, just to see how long she could maintain a pout with his tongue in her mouth.

"I'm sorry. I'll behave," he swore, one hand in the air.

"Don't try to manage me," she muttered. "I know managing when I see it, and *you're* trying to manage me."

"Never." Damon slapped his hand over his chest, shuffling at high speed to keep up. He bent over to look her straight in the eye, fluttering his lashes like an innocent youth. "Unless you like to be managed, because then, hell, yeah."

Her lips twitched. "Just remember I have a job to do, and while I'm happy you're here, I hope this wasn't a mistake."

Something blurred in his peripheral vision, and Damon whirled, moving instinctively to protect her.

Alastair had popped out of nowhere and was pacing at their side. "Oh, dear." He slunk forward, glancing between them, his gaze calculating. "I hope there's no trouble between you two lovebirds."

Damon mentally reviewed what they'd been talking about and how long the cat might have been eavesdropping. He didn't think they'd let anything slip, but a change of topic was probably wise. "It's an impressive building. Your home."

Alastair all but fell over himself getting closer to Damon, adjusting his suit jacket as if he were going on camera. "It's been in the family since the fifteenth century when the Sterling-Wylde clan became lords of the entire area."

"There's an interesting historical significanc—" Addie began, only to be cut off by Alastair.

"Interesting? *Ha*, only if you find death and destruction entertaining. It's one thing to rule, but there've been dark times in our past, and now it's all coming back to haunt us."

The longer he spoke, the more melodramatic he grew and the less worried Damon got. "Haunted. You mean like really haunted?"

"Death curses and the like, yes." Alastair gestured to the wall beside them and the enormous portraits hanging on the twenty-foot-high space. The people in them seemed more ferocious than the ones Damon had seen earlier. "The Wylde side of the family. Our great-grandsire pillaged the manor then claimed the previous Lord Sterling's daughter as his bride. *That's* where the trouble came in, and that's why everything is falling apart. Once I take ownership and the castle is mine, I'm going to do the only thing possible to remove the curse."

If spooky music had started playing at that moment, Damon couldn't have been more delighted. "Does it involve sage fires and secret rituals?"

Alastair offered him a dirty look. "This is so far beyond just the building. It's our *family* that's been cursed, and I don't need this anchor around my neck as I attempt to turn our fortunes around. No, the only way to stop our family name from descending into the depths of ignominy is to get rid of everything. Sell the trinkets, tear down the castle—"

"Oh, please, you're not at this *again* are you, Alastair?" They'd entered the formal dining room where a central table at least thirty feet long was surrounded by massive chairs. Off to one end, places had been set for four. Niall was already seated at the head, adjusting his dress robes as he stared at his brother in disapproval. "It's not good for my digestion to have to constantly listen to you rant about fairytales."

Alastair marched forward, shaking his finger Niall's face. "It's not good for my blood pressure for you ignore the facts. As long as Sterling-Wylde stands, we'll never be free."

Damon wished he had popcorn. He placed a hand on Addie's lower back as he guided her toward the two chairs on the same side of the table, positioning her away from the brothers. "It sounds as if you've got a different idea about how things work, Niall."

The man sniffed. "I have the *right* idea. There is no curse. It's simply bad business management. Once I have official ownership of the estate, I'll turn things around soon enough."

Alastair dropped into the chair across from them and proceeded to scoop spoon after spoon of sugar into his coffee cup while he refused to meet his brother's eye. "You could try, if the curse doesn't kill you first. Besides, there's nothing that says *you're* going to get ownership."

"We agreed not to discuss this topic since it's out of our hands for the time being. But because..." Niall glanced at Damon disapprovingly, sniffing again, "...Addie's boyfriend asked, let me share my plans for the future."

Addie played with her utensils, a small sigh escaping her. Damon glanced over in concern, but she smiled before rolling her eyes as Niall began.

"This manor is a grand and glorious example of our history, and its bounty needs to be shared with current generations. Once I've done some restorations, it'll be a veritable playground again. Just like in the old days when royalty came to hunt, and fish, and when wild revelry filled the ballrooms."

"A hotel?" Damon asked.

"Hardly. That implies commoners would be allowed, whereas it will be for only the most genteel and refined of clientele. We'll cater to the rich and famous from around the world, and once again the Sterling-Wylde name will be exalted in our rightful company." Niall tucked a linen napkin into the heavy brocade necktie around his neck. "Although I don't expect *you* to understand. This is obviously far above you."

Good grief. *The boys*, as Addie called them, were annoying assholes *and* condescending pricks at the same time. He knew why she'd sighed if this was the claptrap she'd had to listen to for the past week.

Of course, what to do about it? Damon grinned. Condescending assholes were the best kind to poke fun at without them realizing it. "I'm sure I don't, but both your plans sound exciting, and I promise to do anything I can to help. I mean, I came here to see Addie, but this is *bigger* than just us. This is something I feel I should be involved in, and it could change my life *forever*."

So he was laying it on a little thick, but he was having too much fun to stop.

Both brothers stared at him, Alastair with a faintly mistrusting look and Niall with sheer calculated mischief.

"I like your attitude," Niall announced.

"I do too," Alastair agreed quickly. "If you want to be involved, we could use your help."

Niall tossed his brother a dirty look. "I was going to suggest that."

"But I said it first."

"He'll work in the gardens," Niall announced.

"What a waste of resources. This is the problem with you, brother, you think too small." Alastair gestured toward Damon. "He's like half of a brute squad all by himself. Addie asked the other day for help moving things. I say we hire Damon to do all the heavy lifting."

"Oh, you would hire me? Like, pay me money and everything?" Damon prattled. "Is that legal, though, because I—"

"Of course. Cash every week, along with room and board," Niall offered. "No one else needs to know about it."

"Wow. I never thought about that. That's *brilliant*," Damon gushed before Addie gave his thigh a sharp pinch. Her eyes were brighter than usual, and she was shaking as she clung to the arms of her chair, leaning back to allow the servant girl to place breakfast in front of her. "What do you say, sweetheart? Don't you think it's a great idea for me to be your helper?"

He gave her his best puppy dog eyes, and she shook harder, swallowing before she spoke. "If Alastair and Niall hire you, I'm sure I can find things for you to do."

"Fabulous. Then it's all decided," Niall proclaimed before digging into his plate of food.

Damon was too hungry to ignore the bounty in front of him, but it was satisfaction for other reasons that kept a smile on his face as he attacked the sausage and eggs. Having an official job gave him an excuse to stick close to Addie at all times. Plus, it might earn him some brownie points, him no longer being an unemployed bum, and all. He'd caught her look of disapproval when she'd thought he'd had no job.

Yup, the trip might have begun as a rescue mission, but

now? It was going to be a hell of a lot of fun. Damon was good with that. He liked fun.

He just had to convince Addie to have some with him.

3

———

She'd admit to being fairly entertained while Damon bantered with the boys at breakfast. He obviously didn't take anything too seriously, not even himself, but he also packed enough shifter power that one direct look and her hosts had backed off post-meal, leaving them alone to head to the gentlemen's parlor to start her workday.

That was a couple of hours ago, and for the first time since the boys had returned to Sterling-Wylde, she was thoroughly enjoying herself.

Not having to worry about the Highland Tigers meant she'd thrown herself into her assignment, completely focused on the task at hand, which was cataloging the filled-to-the-brim den-slash-smoking room.

The job was soothing as she methodically worked her way around the room and added items to the master inventory. She was good at what she did, which was why she was hired for so many high-profile jobs. She went way beyond just creating a list. She categorized items into dynasties, reigning families and historic sections of the household.

She didn't move anything without returning the object to where she'd found it. In one matter, Niall was correct. Sterling-Wylde had been poorly run in the past few years. There were items from the dining room scattered everywhere, and even articles that belonged in the stables tossed up on the walls, probably because the Lord Sterling-Wylde had enjoyed looking at them.

As far as she was concerned, things were meant to be used, but if the manor really was going to be enjoyed by the masses, it needed a lot of work first.

Something fell to the floor, and a metallic ping was followed by a soft curse.

Okay, so she hadn't been one hundred percent focused on her task the entire time. There'd been a large, sexy, wonderful-smelling...*distraction* in the room.

"Please don't touch the horseshoe," she repeated for the umpteenth time. The touching bit, not the horseshoe. That part was new.

"What *can* I touch?" Damon asked in a bit of a huff. "I'm supposed to help you, but so far the only thing I've moved is a chair."

"Don't worry, you'll have plenty of chances to flex your muscles. This just isn't a place where I need physical help." She walked over and firmly pulled the metal U from his hands. Addie crossed the room to the cigar humidor and propped the decorative horseshoe back in its original position displayed on top. "You are helping, really, just by being here. Normally by now one or the other of the boys would have stopped in and stuck around long enough to make me uneasy."

Damon eyed her, his face twisted strangely.

"They never did anything, it's just awkward to have them—"

"It's not that. I get it, they're creepy, but they never crossed the line." He swung his thumb toward her. "How did you know where I got the horseshoe?"

"I have a good memory," she said dryly, pacing back to where she'd left her iPad. Her comment got her a nod, but she recognized his new expression. He had no idea what she was saying.

"Is there anything else I can do to help you?" Damon all but begged. "You want a drink? Are you hungry? How about I sing to you?"

Lordy, she hoped she wouldn't have to entertain him the entire time. "Are you always this annoying?"

"This isn't annoying," he insisted. "This is charming. Flirtatious, even."

He gave her a come-hither look, and she choked on her own spit. "Don't do that again," she ordered.

Damon flopped into the nearest chair (*Item 1511: sixteenth century, mahogany legs, twill cushion; reign of James VI.*) "Don't you ever take coffee breaks?"

"Not often," she admitted. "Since I work by myself, I pretty much put in my time for the day and then stop."

"God, snap that whip a little harder," he muttered. "Why does everyone I know have to be a workaholic?"

"You obviously hang around good people."

"ADHD people. But here's a solution. We'll take a coffee break right here." Damon glanced around the room, his face lighting up as he spotted something. "I challenge you to a game of chess."

"You're a glutton for punishment." Addie turned back to work, opening a new document on her iPad for the antique pipes stored in a display case on the wall.

"Oh, come on," he taunted. "I promise to go easy on you. I'll spot you a couple pieces."

He had no idea what trouble he was getting into. "I don't think—"

"It'll be fun. I promise. Trust me, Addie, I know how to make things fun." He drifted closer, his bright eyes fixed on her as she eased away.

Her wolf wanted to come out to meet him. Heck, her human side wanted to lick him up one side and down the other. Being watched by the Sterling-Wylde boys had never produced this effect in her.

Straight up, Damon turned her on.

But Addie gave herself a stern lecture. This was not the time, and most certainly *not* the place, and even though mutual attraction shone clearly in his eyes, fooling around would be too complicated. She didn't need complicated.

Only while she'd been coming to a firm decision and bracing herself to turn him down, Damon had closed the gap between them. Small steps, stalking her. Herding her away from the delicate display case without her being aware of it until her back bumped into a solid wood-paneled wall.

His eyes flickered between human and shifter, his nostrils flaring as he edged in closer. "There's something about you... Are you sure we haven't met before? At some party, maybe?"

She worked to keep her breathing steady. Her pulse she could do nothing about, its frantic, out-of-control beat giving her away even as she forced herself to project a façade of serenity.

His breathing accelerated. Whatever was happening, he felt it too.

"I doubt we travel in the same social circles," she said as calmly as possible.

"We should. We totally should. Like later, let me take you out on the town. You can show me what there is to do on a hot summer night in the Scottish Highlands." He planted both hands on the wall, one on either side of her head before taking a long, slow breath, his eyes closing as he scented her.

Not good. It was not good the way her legs shook, and her palms were sweaty, and her strongest desire wasn't to get her job done but to take him back to her room, strip them down and produce some heat of their own.

"Queen's rook to E4," she whispered.

He blinked, and the silver-grey in his eyes changed back to vivid blue. "What?"

"Queen's rook to E4."

Damon paused. "*Really?*"

She nodded. "You move the pieces, though. I need to keep working."

He shook himself and stepped away, his body's reaction to the desire between them clear in the tent rising behind his blue kilt. He offered her a final cocky smile then gave her breathing room. She frantically sucked in air to stop her head from spinning, knees locked to keep from falling over.

"Give me a second to get the board ready," Damon offered, moving the antique marble chess men into position, sitting behind the desk with the black pieces toward him. He glanced up. "You're going to work while we play?"

She wasn't going any closer. Not right now, because not even the desk between them was enough of a barrier. "Why? Do you not understand what move I called?"

His eyes narrowed at her challenge. "Let's wager on the game."

"Deal. If I win, you don't ask me to play again."

"That's not a wager. Best two out of three, and the winner gets a massage."

"Best two out of three, and the winner gets the bed," she offered.

He looked stunned. "You're the weirdest girlfriend I've ever had."

Addie laughed. "Make your move, buddy."

She went back to the case and jotted down the next bit of information.

Item 1512: Inlaid turquoise, with a cherry bowl; one of a set (reference page 37).

Item 1513: bowl made of tusk, oxen; maple shaft.

She glanced at the chessboard. "Queen to F3."

"My rook takes yours." Damon switched the pieces. "Are you really going to keep working?"

"Bishop to C4. Don't worry, we'll be done soon enough."

He grunted suspiciously then made her move, pondering the board for longer this time before he jumped a knight. She called her response as she wrote down *Item 1515: bowl ash; chestnut shaft.* The rest of the game didn't take long. She'd glance at the board, offer a move, then work until Damon called her name.

Announcing, "Castle to D8. Checkmate," was fairly anticlimactic.

Damon leaned back in his chair as a grunt of surprise escaped him. "Damn it, I forgot about your bishop sitting there. Well played. Ready for round two?"

The second time it took her ten moves to lock him in position. By then she was also done with the pipes, opening a new page in her inventory and stepping toward the window—

—and bouncing off a rock-solid body she swore hadn't

been there a moment earlier. He caught her before she tumbled to the ground, his hands warm on her sleeves, and she hesitated briefly before easing from his grasp.

"Explain how you did that," Damon demanded.

"I told you," she said. "I have a good memory. As in a really, *really* good memory. As soon as you made a move, I thought back to the chess games I'd read about, found one that matched, then proceeded to copy the winning moves. Congrats, by the way. We reenacted a game from nineteen fifty-eight."

Damon's grin returned. "Well, colour me embarrassed. And good for you. I see why this job is perfect. The inventory business, I mean."

"I like it. Keeps me out of mischief, and the pay is good."

"Except sometimes you have to work around people you don't trust."

He was right, but she did have ways to protect herself. She just didn't like to use them unless she had to.

And now that the game was over, he was back in her airspace. "I can open these drawers all by myself," she said firmly.

"But I like helping you," he rumbled, wrapping his fingers around her forearm and caressing.

She fought the rush of desire, locking down her system so her wolf didn't do something stupid like offer her neck. "You know what? A coffee sounds good—could you get me one? Cream and sugar. Thanks. And maybe something to eat."

She whirled and headed in the opposite direction, talking out loud as she pretended to count pictures on the walls, taking copious notes.

She knew *he* knew she'd invented an excuse to get rid of

him, but he didn't say anything, slipping from the room after offering one final confused glance.

Addie collapsed into a chair and let out a long, slow breath. She didn't know who was more agitated, her or her wolf. She hadn't wanted complicated. Tough luck.

It seemed *complicated* had arrived, and his name was Damon.

~

DAMON PRECARIOUSLY BALANCED two coffees and a scone as he stared in confusion at the identical stone-lined hallways in front of him leading off in different directions.

It was his third time returning from the kitchens, and he'd made it a personal challenge to take a different route every time. Coming back with coffee that morning had been a straightforward trip. Lunch—he'd gotten turned around once before finding his way. Addie nodded her thanks then proceeded to eat her sandwich one-handed as she continued to work.

This time he'd found a side passage off a side passage, but after working his way through a labyrinth of stone, he was no closer to where he needed to be and getting antsy at having been gone for too long.

The lingering scents were muted, as if he'd stumbled upon a rarely used section of the manor, and from the thick layer of dust everywhere, that was probably true. The only thing visible underfoot was a set of oversized prints. Not big enough for a tiger, but definitely a cat, especially after he'd followed them a ways and discovered a pile of mouse carcasses.

Maybe he wouldn't bring Addie on this route anytime soon.

He hurried down the passageway, jerking to a stop as it dead-ended at a plain, wooden barrier.

"Hell." There had to be a way out. Damon leaned on the wall with a shoulder, jumping back as it swung to the right to reveal a familiar carpeted foyer. He rushed forward, glancing back as the secret door closed behind him with a soft sigh.

Yup, this place was full of surprises. Like the enormous housecat pretending to be a statue on the antique sideboard, a dark shadow falling across its body and partially hiding it from sight.

Damon didn't give a rip if there were a million cats in the house stalking him at this point; he wanted to get back to Addie. To protect her, yes, but more as well. No matter how much he told himself to cool it, his craving for her grew stronger.

He ignored the oversized cat when it jumped to the carpet as he passed, its feet hitting the floor with a gentle thump. Damon strode forward, considering his powerful case of possessiveness as he closed the distance on his target.

He was strong enough to lead his own pack, but hadn't wanted the responsibility, so going lone wolf years ago had seemed the smartest choice. But hanging around Addie for most of the day had done something bizarre to his system. He knew what it was like to feel protective—he'd always had that instinct in spades. He was here to keep her safe.

This was about something else. Something...deeper. Maybe?

One decision was simple. Although his wolf was acting capital-W weird, Damon would do what was right. He'd take care of Addie, whatever that looked like.

Ahead of him, he caught a glimpse of a dark pant leg disappearing around the corner. He sped up, his feet narrowly missing the cat that slipped in front of him. It swerved at the last moment, hissing before dashing out of reach back down the hallway.

He moved more cautiously, catching Alastair leaning against the exterior wall of the smoking room, one eye pressed nearly to the wooden paneling. Damon snuck up until he was behind the man, then coughed.

Alastair flew upward, spinning in midair before landing with his hands raised, claws out. He blinked hard before jerking upright. His furious, fearful glare switching to his arrogant one. "Damon."

"Alastair. Can I help you?"

The man shook his head, shuffling sideways until he was no longer between Damon and the wall. "Thought I'd stop by to see how you and Addie were getting along." He smiled, but the expression never reached his eyes. "It takes a certain kind of man to handle a woman like her."

As if implying Damon wasn't that kind of man. The insinuation wasn't the most annoying part, though. Damon gave zero fucks what Alastair thought of him. The idea of the other man *handling* Addie, or any woman for that matter...

Alastair and guys like him were the reason castration had been invented.

So Damon didn't answer. Just stood in place and stared and stared until the other man cleared his throat, pivoted on the spot and paced away as if he weren't scared to death.

Damon waited until the echoes of Alastair's footsteps fell silent before examining the wall more closely. The section was covered with elaborate carvings, and he put down the coffee cups to find what he was looking for.

There, at eye height, was a spyhole. A small section of

paneling slid aside and offered a view into the room. Alastair *had* been watching Addie work.

Creepy, she'd said. Downright freaky, as far as Damon was concerned.

He slipped into the room without telling her what he'd discovered. After how jittery he'd made her that morning, and with her already being concerned about the boys' stalker tendencies, he figured he'd save it for a better moment.

"Coffee?"

Addie smiled as she took the drink. "That took a while. You run into any ghosts out there?"

Not unless ghosts wore Armani. "Nope. Nothing interesting at all."

He retreated to a corner, staying out of her way as much as possible to watch her work for the rest of the afternoon.

She moved so smoothly it was as if she danced around the room, shifting aside one object to examine the one behind it. Or she'd pick up a statue or a plate to check the bottom, but more often than not she simply looked. Her big whisky-coloured eyes would land on an object, then she'd blink, her lips would twitch into a smile, and she'd make a note.

Sometimes it took less than a second. The longest was about ten. She was absolutely amazing, and Damon found her mesmerizing.

When the alarm on her watch went off, she glanced at her wrist in surprise before her shoulders curled forward and she exhaled, a happy sound. It was one he'd like to hear over and over, especially if he were the one getting her to voice her pleasure.

It was the longest Damon'd sat in one place for ages, but

it had been an enjoyable afternoon. Watching her—something about it was so right. "You must be tired."

"Oh!" She whirled, her hand flying to her chest for a second. "I forgot you were there."

"Good. That means I wasn't bothering you."

She shook her head before stretching, linking her fingers together and reaching for the ceiling. "You were fine."

Damon let his gaze drift over her gentle curves as her dark brown sweater stretched in intriguing ways. He longed to go over and give her a rub. He'd start at her shoulders and neck, then work his way down to more sensitive spots. He could make her forget about those aching muscles for a bit and—

His wolf snapped a warning, and he jerked his gaze away before she noticed. *What the heck?* After staying hidden all day, now his beast chose to interfere? And it was pretty clear what his other half was thinking. His wolf didn't want her frightened or upset again by *his* actions.

Great. His animal side was giving him lessons in manners.

He rose and moved toward Addie, mindful to keep his body language casual. "Please tell me we don't have to eat dinner with the conspiracy twins," he begged.

She laughed. "You're safe. The cook has been leaving me a cold supper in the fridge. I asked at breakfast if she'd leave extra for you. Or, you know, you're welcome to cook for us."

"I can cook. I cook great," Damon responded so quickly she raised a brow before breaking into a soft laugh.

Damn it, if he wagged his tail a little harder she might pet his puppy, and that wasn't a euphemism for anything. He just felt...out of sorts all of a sudden. Out of sorts and yet desperate for her approval.

She gestured toward the door. "Why don't you lead the way? It's a big house. I'll feel better once I know you won't get lost."

"*Aww*, you're worried about me."

"Of course. The way Alastair talks, sinister beings wait around every corner to lure you to your death. And Niall —?" She shook her head. "Sometimes when he talks about restoring the place to its ancient glory, I wonder if he means to include the dungeons."

Interesting. He held the door for her then caught up, guiding her without touching even though he wanted to take her hand. "I explored when I was out earlier. The manor does need work."

Anything to keep the conversation rolling. If all he got was to listen to her voice, he'd take it.

"Repairs? It does, but spending the money and time to fix it up only for the one percent to enjoy?" A heavy sigh escaped her. "It would be a shame to burn it down, as well."

Damon took a side passage, different than the one he'd discovered coming back with their coffees. "So, tell me. What would you do with a Scottish castle if you had one?"

"Are you giving me a Scottish castle?" she asked, her lighthearted tease thrilling him. She gestured at the passing windows, and the rich greens and vivid blues outside. "Sterling-Wylde is in such an idyllic setting, and with the lake and the woods nearby, it would make a beautiful retreat. A place for lone wolves, or solitary bears. Fox shifters without partners—that kind of thing."

"You'd fill it with recluses."

"Yes, and no. Shifters who need space, because there's enough room here to get away and yet stay in contact with others. That's important." She glanced at him, something all too knowing in her eyes. "Even lone wolves need others."

Damon didn't answer because anything he said might give him away. He wondered if maybe his friend Jim had told her details about him, but as they grabbed dinner from the fridge to take to their room, he remembered her earlier confusion regarding his job situation and knew that hadn't been faked.

She knew about him; she didn't *know* him. Yet she had figured out something personal just from being in the same room all day.

Was he as easy to catalog as an heirloom pipe?

They remained silent on the trip from the kitchen to the tower room where Damon set their tray of food and drink on the balcony table. The sun was a long ways from setting, still high above the mountains, its light casting a golden tint to the sky. The glow reflected on the surface of the water, turning the lake to a shimmering mirror. Magical, especially when he added in the peaceful noises around them. Birds, and crickets, and little critters wrestling in the long grass.

Addie put down her spoon and closed her eyes, taking a deep breath as she cocked her head to the side and listened to the cooing doves. "Just think if stressed-out, hurried people got to soak this in for a while. It could do them a whole lot of good." She opened her eyes and offered him a faint smile. "It does *me* good. I like my job, but you're right about my bad habit. I never take coffee breaks, or things like that. I tend to work straight through, although I do refresh myself in the evening."

He couldn't resist any longer. He laid a hand over her fingers, a flash of heat rolling up his arm as if he'd touched a live wire. "Addie—"

She jerked her hand away, placing it in her lap, her fingers locked together as she stared over the railing away from him. "I meant to ask earlier. To confirm there's no problem with you staying on for a while?"

"I am your humble servant." He said it without a trace of sarcasm. In fact if anything, there was far too much other emotion in the words, as if it were impossible to resist letting her know how much he wanted her.

Damon's wolf snapped at him again.

He backed off though he longed to go around the table and pull her into his arms. To tilt her chin back, press their lips together and take another taste. The light reflected on her skin, turning her all warm and soft in the setting sun, and what he wanted most of all was to—

His wolf vanished.

Between one second and the next the other part of him that had always been around threw up its paws and pulled into the deepest recesses of his mind. Damon clutched the table, trying to catch his balance. Trying to understand and deal with the strange lack inside.

"Are you okay?" Addie leaned closer. "What's wrong?"

He shook his head. "Indigestion. Excuse me."

He escaped to the bathroom, desperate to figure out what had just happened. He stared into the mirror and watched his eyes as he attempted to summon the other part of himself.

He couldn't do it. He couldn't pull his wolf to the foreground.

The beast was still there, hiding as it pouted. "Good grief, what the hell is wrong with you?" Damon demanded, glaring at himself and thinking how incredibly stupid he must look.

Sending out a shot of Alpha power did absolutely nothing. He hadn't expected it to since that was basically like arguing with himself. He stripped down and tried to force a change, but his wolf snapped back and told him to go away. He didn't feel sick, but maybe this was the start of some exotic and rare wasting disease contracted by being doused in Scottish swamp water at a cursed castle.

His wolf popped up for just a moment to offer the assurances that *they aren't sick* and *this isn't forever*, and then the beast shut down so hard Damon's ears rang.

He'd barely finished pulling his clothes back on when a hesitant knock sounded on the door. He opened it to discover Addie's gorgeous brow was creased with concern as her gaze darted over him.

"Are you sure you're all right?"

There was nothing else to be done. Damon lied his ass off. "It's jet lag. Time to turn in."

Addie nodded, backing into the room. She cast a nervous glance at the bed before smiling sweetly. "Make yourself comfortable. I'm going to read for a few hours before I call it a day."

He couldn't believe his ears. "You're not making me sleep on the couch?"

She shook her head. "Number one, I basically cheated to beat you at chess, and two, you would never fit. The couch was built in seventeen forty-two, and you're far too tall."

Damon had no energy to gloat over his good luck in being taller than the eighteenth-century castle occupants. He barely had enough strength to offer a protest.

"I'm not letting you sleep on it. I'll take the floor."

"Take the bed," Addie insisted. "I'll...join you later. It'll be fine."

She was full of surprises, and if he weren't about to fall over he would have had more to say. He'd pulled the jet-lag ticket, but a wave of true exhaustion had hit, so he stripped off his borrowed kilt and linen shirt, tossing them over the heavy wooden support at the foot of the bed. "I promise I'll wake up if you need me. If the ghosts or the boys come calling, I'll protect you."

His head barely hit the pillow before utter exhaustion dragged him under, and while he kept his word and stayed moderately alert, the only thing that brought him to attention was nearly four hours later when Addie jumped on the bed in her wolf form, turning around twice before settling at his side.

Beautiful, smart, *clever* woman. Damon was impressed even as he was thoroughly perplexed.

What the hell was his wolf doing?

4

———

*D*amon slowly came awake to the awareness his fingers were tangled in soft fur. The dim light of dawn was creeping into the corners of the massive room, but it was bright enough for him to see the dark wolf curled against him.

A quick glance at the clock on the sideboard showed it was just after four a.m. Two windows of the tower room faced east, and soon the chamber would be filled with sunshine. Astonished he'd slept as long as he had, some of his absolute relaxation had to do with the woman sleeping peacefully in her shifted form at his side.

He leaned up on an elbow, curious to examine her closer. Such a beautiful black wolf, with little white socks on her front paws. Damon could picture her hitting them against the ground to get his attention or batting him playfully. He reached inside himself to figure out what the heck was wrong with his wolf. The beast simply rolled over once before declaring everything was fine as far as he was concerned, but he wasn't going to show up anytime soon.

Funny how that wasn't very reassuring...

Today while he watched Addie, Damon would check the Internet to see if there'd ever been mention of others experiencing an internal wolf rebellion. He didn't want to alert anyone something might be wrong. He didn't want his family to freak out, but maybe this was worthy of freak-out territory. His wolf was a big part of him, and for the beast to go into hiding—there had to be a damn good reason.

And as much as he wanted to stay in bed and keep staring at the pretty little wolf beside him, he needed to burn off some energy.

He checked his clothes in the bathroom where he'd hung them to dry, but the jeans had seen better days. They'd been ripped to shreds along one leg so that when he pulled them on, he looked like the tramp the Sterling-Wylde boys thought he was. Normally he'd shift into his wolf to go for a run, but that option wasn't available at the moment.

Well, he'd dealt with worse. Damon reached for another kilt and linen shirt, laughing softly as he pulled them on. It seemed he was going local for the next while. At least, if he did meet a ghost or two, he'd fit right in.

He locked the door after one final glance at Addie's form on the bed, her ribs rising and falling in a peaceful rhythm as she slumbered on. Then he made his way outside where he took off his boots and wiggled his toes in the dew-wet grass, the manicured lawn before him stretching into the distance. Groomed trees lay to his right and the lake to his left, and he started slowly before breaking into a full-out run, pushing his body hard.

As weird as his wolf was acting, he was glad he was here. He'd hated to see the anxiety in Addie's eyes, and if nothing else, he had no objection to sticking around to make her job easier. His heart pounded as he ran, but other than his wolf being an ass, physically he felt fine. He was sure he could protect her even with whatever was wrong with him.

Damon ran for an hour until the sun peeked over the nearest hillock, casting long shadows as it filtered through the trees. The sky grew brighter, and the world around him turned into a fantasyland of pixie dust and Scottish legend.

He'd looped around the perimeter of the estate and was nearing the watchtower by the southern entrance when he came across a small gate in the tall rock wall. The door was ajar, and he peeked through to discover a group of thatched cottages, smoke pouring from the chimneys. A young man worked a rake outside one of them. He must've sensed Damon because he glanced up and their eyes met. The worker waved then beckoned him over.

Damon sauntered forward, taking in the flowers and the neat garden area. The scent of shifter greeted him as well, and he smiled.

Highland Tigers, and now foxes, or some combination thereof.

"Are you lost?" the man asked, eyeing Damon's bare feet and clothing, but he didn't look judgmental. Just smiled and spoke hospitably. "If you've gotten turned around, I can get you back to the manor."

"You work here?"

He nodded, brushing the dirt from his hand on one thigh before extending it to Damon. "Glenn Chappie. I'm in charge of the gardens and lawns. My grandmam is the cook at the manor. If you'd like to come in for a cuppa, we'll be heading over in a bit. You can walk with us."

Damon didn't bother to explain he wasn't lost. Instead, he admired the neat little village and the obvious signs of Glenn's green thumb. "Does everyone who lives here work for the Sterling-Wyldes?"

Glenn opened the door to the cottage and called in a warning. "Grandmam. We have a guest." He turned back to Damon to motion him in. "All of us in the holding do, yes. Some have been employed for generations, helping care for the manor. Years ago more servants worked and lived on-site."

Damon stepped through the door into the presence of a petite fox-shifter bent nearly double with age. Only when he looked into her eyes, they were bright and shining, clear as starlight. She was as close as foxes got to an Alpha, he suspected. Not up to *his* caliber, but powerful in her own way. She looked him over for a good long time, Glenn standing at her side, and his wolf stirred. Damon moved cautiously, not wanting to frighten either of them.

She wasn't afraid. She fixed him in place like his father had when he'd been young and in trouble. "Are ye the one who caused all the ruckus at the manor yesterday?" she demanded.

"Possibly?" he admitted, highly entertained by her careful enunciation. There was a bit of broad Scots in her voice, but she was easy to understand. "You're the one responsible for the delicious food in the pantry."

She nodded, beaming at his compliment. "You'll be staying, then. You'll let me know some of your favourites, and I'll see what I can do."

Glenn whistled lightly in appreciation, patting Damon on the back as he stepped past. "Clever devil. How did you get on her good side so quickly?"

Grandmam reached out her age-worn fingers and, with the cockiness of a woman who knows exactly how esteemed she is, pinched Damon's cheek. "He's a good lad. Strong, and eager to do what's right."

Damon wasn't sure he wanted such glowing accolades

pointed in his direction, but she just gave him another approving nod then filled plates for him and Glenn. They sat at the small table as the sun rose and the day officially began, chatting all the while about the goings-on at the manor.

Damon listened with interest, keeping an eye on the clock on the wall to make sure he got back to the manor in time to escort Addie safely to work.

It was still early when they'd cleaned up and headed across the wide green expanse toward the Sterling-Wylde keep. Grandmam leaned on the arm of an old man Damon remembered seeing pacing the halls, some kind of glorified butler.

"A warning." Glenn spoke privately as he kept an eye on the two walking ahead of them. "You caught Grandmam in one of her more lucid moments. If the next time you bump into her she doesn't remember you, don't take it personally."

Ahhh. "Alzheimer's? Or just old age?"

"Nothing that's been diagnosed, and she's not in any danger, but she forgets people. Forgets the connections." Glenn pulled out his wallet and showed the pictures he carried with him. "When I need to, I use these to nudge her memory. She remembers every recipe she ever learned, but sometimes she calls me Roger, which was my father's name. And sometimes she thinks I'm a guest visiting during the heyday of the early 1930s."

"She's seen a lot of history," Damon said. "Don't worry. I'll treat her with the respect she clearly deserves. I think it's wonderful she still gets to work at the manor."

Glenn made a rude noise. "At least until the will is settled. At that point, we'll all be turned out on our ears, no matter which one of the sons inherits."

Damon stuttered to a halt, ready to ask questions, when it struck him. "Alastair wants to burn everything to the ground. Niall wants to turn the place into a high-class retreat—and neither of those call for an old woman and her family to continue to work in the place they've lived their entire lives."

The gardener shrugged as he acknowledged Damon's guess. "In some ways I agree with Alastair. It might hurt less to simply have the place gone than to have to see other people running our home."

They were at a fork in the path, and Damon paused. "There's something I want to check before I go in, but it was good to meet you."

Glenn tipped his hat and offered a toothy smile. "Good to meet you too. Anyone Grandmam likes is a quality person."

He took his leave, catching up with the rest of the crowd strolling toward the manor.

Damon turned in the opposite direction into the small castle-like structure with a gated wall stretching over the path. He drifted along, and his wolf—*hallelujah!*—snuck out of hiding as he explored the watchtower.

He'd felt off balance with the beast completely out of reach.

The stone citadel wasn't used any longer, but it was in decent shape, and he climbed the spiral staircase to the top, gazing out the window across to the room in the turret where he'd spent the night with Addie.

Something rumbled inside, and it wasn't his stomach. No, it was anticipation on his wolf's part. He wanted to see her again.

Damn beast was going to drive him mad.

"Make up your bloody mind," he muttered at...well, at

himself. "You're the one who took off, not me," he reminded his wolf. "*No scaring her*, remember?"

His wolf sniffed in disdain as if it were tired of trying to explain a concept as convoluted as quantum physics to a three-year-old.

Damon took the stairs down two at a time, jerking to a halt at a shadow moving in his peripheral vision. His wolf perked up its ears as he breathed in, the scent of cat triggering the instinct to track and hunt.

Another large striped house cat darted from behind the rock wall, and Damon grinned. One of the local mousers must live in the watchtower. He trailed it until it vanished. One second it was there, the next it was gone, and it took Damon actually running his hand over the wall to find the optical illusion—a rock pillar set narrowly away from the main wall that covered the entrance to a smooth tunnel heading downward and toward the manor.

She knew what a coward looked like.

Addie paced the hallway and ignored the telltale signs of her uneasy sleep that were far too visible in the mirrors she passed on the way to the parlor.

She was grateful Damon had been gone when she dragged her carcass from the bed. She'd spent the entire evening refusing to admit her attraction to the mischievous shifter.

Slipping into her wolf form and putting a barrier between them wasn't wrong. It just wasn't what she really wanted, and taking the easy way out made her mad for so many reasons.

Sex had become complicated. She wasn't an Omega

wolf—not a full one—but she'd inherited an empathetic talent from her dual Omega parents. Over the years that gift had gone haywire, until the past months, when she touched others, she found herself drowning in emotion. *Their* emotions.

It made being intimate difficult, to say the least.

It didn't make the fact she ached to get up close and personal with Damon any less real. It did make the depth of her desire that much more mysterious.

She was distracted enough with her thoughts that she was all the way into the smoking room before she froze, pivoting slowly at the eerie sensation between her shoulder blades. That feeling she was being watched was back in full force. If she'd discovered Alastair perched on the top of a bookcase, she wouldn't have been surprised.

Creeped out, but not surprised.

Only there was no Highland Tiger. And no Damon, although she expected he'd show up eventually. Addie did a single loop through the room, sniffing to find a hint of something that would justify her discomfort. But while she scented the boys, Damon and herself, all of the scents were older and mingled together.

Clearly her lack of sleep was causing paranoia.

She turned back to face the door, standing at the edge of the fireplace as she prepared to start work for the day.

The faintest of creaks sounded. She reached down without looking, picked up the wrought-iron poker from beside the fireplace, and spun with full force toward the intruder suddenly standing behind her.

A flash of blond hair was all she saw before her assailant ducked, the poker continuing on to strike the heavy bricks of the fireplace. The sharpened side point dug in, capturing her weapon and rendering it useless.

"Stop—"

She kept twirling, letting go of the poker but clenching her fists together until she made contact with a solid male jaw. And then she was falling, with a stranger's hands gripping her wrists, her body twisting as he took her down with him.

A moment later they hit the ground with her on top, impact knocking a grunt from them both. Addie found herself rolled to the carpet, her hands pinned to the floor by an ironclad grasp. A much heavier body over hers made it impossible to move.

"—Addie. It's *me*, Damon."

It had only been seconds. She gazed up into sky-blue eyes, and suddenly her rapid heartbeat wasn't from the adrenaline rush, or fear. His gaze dropped to her lips, and she found herself holding her breath. Waiting. Wanting.

His eyes shimmered, a hint of his wolf's silver colouring visible before vanishing completely, but as confusing as that was, she was more focused on the connection between them. On the heavy weight of his hips, on his muscular thighs pushing between hers. On the thickening length of his erection pressing against her belly.

She expected to be bombarded with an emotional overload from him, but the only thing attacking her system was sheer outright lust. And given the strange circumstances, she wasn't about to look the gift wolf in the mouth.

Damon swore softly then met her halfway as they both dove into a kiss marked by more enthusiasm than finesse.

Their lack of restraint didn't make it messy, just made it real. The shifter on top of her had some mad skills, and he used every one of them. Teeth—just enough to set her squirming. Tongue—an enticing promise of how well he could use that talented appendage on other parts of her at a later point. Lips—possessive, yet soft. He set her wrists free, moving to explore her body. Twisting to the side as he skimmed a hand over her lower back and rolled, draping her over his whip-hard body.

His caresses felt amazing, and not nearly enough. He slid a hand under her pants to cup her ass while she discovered both her palms were nestled against his muscular chest. Caution bells went off, the kind that warned if they went beyond this point, they couldn't turn back.

Even though the usual overwhelming rush of emotion wasn't there, she had to stop them. It would be far better to call quits now than if her shitty situation reverted to normal, and she lost control like usual, maybe when he was inside her.

Because *that* would go over oh-so-well.

Lust was one thing, but people's emotions were tricky things. It was never *just* lust. Never just passion...

She wrenched their mouths apart, her wolf mourning the loss, and a sad whimper escaped her human lips. She agreed with her other half. The last thing she wanted right now was to stop.

The instant she pulled away Damon responded, jerking his hands off her as she sat up, straddling his lean hips. He stared wide-eyed as her breathing stuttered like air driven from a billow.

His upper body shook, his pulse beat rapidly in his neck, and oh *God*, she wanted to lean down and put her teeth into him. Sink in and bite him, *hard*, mark him, and though she knew she couldn't—*mustn't*—the urge grew stronger.

The hunger in his eyes was clear, and her body ached

for them to continue what they'd started, but she had to take control. Had to do the right thing.

"I need a notebook," she blurted out. "There are extras in the storage off the music room. Main floor, north of the dining hall."

A crease formed between his brows, but he nodded and pulled himself back from the brink. He stroked his knuckles briefly over her cheek before extracting himself from under her and leaping to his feet. "I can get that for you. I'll be right back."

He was out of the room, the door swinging closed with a loud *snap* as she took a deep breath and worked to settle herself.

She glanced between the opening beside the fireplace and the closed door Damon had vanished behind. Missing wills and secret passages. She had the most intriguing job ever, and she wouldn't trade it for the world, but this *thing* with Damon was a snag she hadn't expected.

She examined the hinges on the secret door, working the locking mechanism until she could reopen it at will from both sides. Then she closed it firmly, wishing she could just as easily close off the wash of emotion and desire still rushing through her veins.

5

———

hirty minutes later, she still hadn't started her day. It was impossible to get anything done. Every time she opened her iPad to add information, the memory of being in Damon's arms would repeat itself and she'd lose all focus.

She found herself seated behind the old lord's desk, staring into space as she daydreamed about Damon's touch, analyzing it for more than what it had done to her body, although, *holy moly*, she had a few thoughts about that topic alone. Her belly still quivered—

Liar.

Okay, fine, she admitted to herself, a touch lower than her belly was where she ached, and if she kept thinking about him for much longer, she'd have a hand between her legs in no time flat to deal with the longings he'd triggered.

No, she had to consider what the kiss *hadn't* done to her. She'd expected to be overwhelmed with emotion. Should have been. Was it just him, or them, or something else altogether?

A glimmer of hope rose. Maybe she was outgrowing the

backlash. Or if the exception to the rule was unique to Damon, that could still work in their favour. If she could touch him without negative repercussions, they could enjoy each other's company in the coming days.

Addie let out a slow breath. She craved touch. The past year because of her *gift*, she hadn't been able to partake in any physical pleasure the way she'd wanted.

She forced herself to get up and start on her next task only because she didn't want to be sitting there like a love-struck, teenaged groupie when Damon returned from his made-up task.

One thing the brief pause had done, though, was let her make a decision. She wasn't ready to jump in with both feet. She *was* ready to shake the tree a few more times and see what fell out. If she did a little cautious touching and had no bad reactions...

The idea might backfire, but it was a whole lot better than her other options. Continuing to say no outright was not enjoyable, but having to stop them again after getting his motor running—nope, slow and steady was the only way to deal with it. Especially since there was potentially a sweet reward in the end.

That decided, she got back to work, an unexpected buzz of energy in her veins as she turned to a new section of the bookcase.

The door opened, and she turned with a happy smile toward Damon, freezing when Niall entered instead, his robes swaying as he moved.

"Can I help you?" she asked warily, eyeing the door behind him. He'd pushed it, but not hard enough, and now it stood open a few inches.

"Possibly." He raised a brow. "Have you found any keys while you've been working?"

He paced closer as he spoke, and Addie ducked away, putting the desk between them as she pretended to consider. She pressed a finger against her lips and glanced skyward before remembering that was a giveaway tell for a lie.

She met his gaze straight on and nodded. "I remember. There are some in the kitchen, and in the garden shed, and I believe—"

"None of those. I need the keys for the anteroom off my father's chambers. His valet insists he can't remember where he put the spare, and I don't want to tear down the wall if I can avoid it."

He spoke with a smile, as if trying to charm her. Maybe someone else would find him attractive, but all she could do was compare him and his brother to Damon and find them wanting. Niall's long hair and elaborate purple robes seemed formal and yet cheesy; Alastair's expensive suits were pretty, but he was stiff and boring. Damon's lighthearted acceptance of the borrowed kilts made him look like a swashbuckling hero, his strong body a plaid-wrapped present.

Addie hurried to refocus. "Of course. I would expect you'd—"

Niall cut her off again, stepping closer and reaching past her to the bookcase at her back. Unless she wanted to make a big deal out of it and crawl across the desktop to get away from him, she was stuck as he pulled forward a small cigar box, holding it between them. "Have you looked in here yet?" he asked, whispering the words.

Were...? Were his eyelashes *fluttering* at her?

Ick.

"No. I like to work the perimeter of each room. I'm actually on that bookcase over there."

She pointed and attempted to dodge around him, but he blocked her way, the scent of cat making her nose twitch.

Niall made a noise deep in his throat as he looked her over. "You're a pretty thing, aren't you?"

"I have a boyfriend," she squeaked, pissed that her words escaped so wimpily, but he'd caught hold of her hand, and in that instant, she'd been deluged.

Her gift? Not gone. Not gone at *all*.

Anger at his brother. Lust for her. Dirty urges, evil thoughts and cruel memories swamped her. It was as if a bucketful of every horrid, putrid emotion Niall had ever felt had been dumped on her head. She couldn't fight back or run from the room. Instead, all her energy was consumed by the urgent need to stay vertical and not fall to the ground unconscious.

"Your boyfriend?" He laughed and the sound rang in her ears, tinny and thin. "Very sweet you're concerned about the pauper, but really, he doesn't have to know," Niall carried on, the slimiest slime in his voice as he stroked a finger over her cheek. She gagged, twisting away. "I've far more to offer you, especially once I'm master of Sterling-Wylde."

Her nausea rose rapidly, and as much as she disliked her options, Addie prepared to defend herself. It would mean the end of her job, but she refused to become a victim. She took a deep breath—

The door slammed against the wall. Niall twirled on the spot just as Damon finished sliding across the desk surface and landed with his feet firmly planted on the ground between the two of them.

He ignored Niall, looking straight into Addie's eyes. "You okay?"

She nodded, unable to speak. Fighting to keep from retching on the spot.

He tilted his head toward the door, and she escaped without a protest. Fresh air hit her, but still her feet moved, and she raced from her fears, positive Damon would come looking for her when he was done with Niall.

She couldn't decide what she hoped *done* would mean —for him to kill the cat, or not.

~

DAMON WAITED until Addie was gone before facing his prey, and make no mistake, Niall was one small step from becoming kitty-shish-kah-bob.

"Was there something you needed?" Damon growled dangerously.

He'd wondered briefly if his wolf acting crazy would leave him at a disadvantage, but he shouldn't have. The beast was back. Not until Addie had left the room, but once it was just him and Niall, his wolf came rushing to just under his skin, sending out warning signals to all the shifters in the area that Damon was large, and in charge, and not to be fucked with.

Niall pulled himself together rapidly, blinking to chase the fear away as his pupils changed from human to cat and back again. "Just needed Addie to find something for me," he purred diplomatically, backing away.

The cat was scared, and he should be. Damon caught hold of his own wrist, spreading and fisting his free hand as if warming up to rip the other man apart. He flexed his biceps as he glared at Niall. Nothing over the line in terms of impropriety, but with plenty of warning in the growled words. "Next time, ask *me*."

Niall darted from the room, leaving Damon alone with all sorts of problematic emotions. The wolf took over, and he threw back his head and let out a frustrated howl. Addie wasn't officially his to protect, but damn if he didn't want her to be, and that was enough to send a shockwave through his system.

He needed a moment to collect himself before he went after her. Whatever had started between them that morning —it was a good thing she'd called them off when she did. First, it would have been pretty crass to make their first time together an out-of-control fuck in the middle of someone else's smoking room. But adding in the whole screwed-up mystery of his wolf's erratic behavior—

Damon was one confused beast.

The good part about his wolf hiding away meant they weren't fighting. Yes, he was a wolf and the wolf was him, but too many times the two sides had different ideas how to solve problems.

And Addie was a problem, all right. A huge, mysterious, *tempting* problem.

He left the room, following her scent to the end of the hall and up the stairs. The closer he got, the stronger the smell of her fear, and the more agitated his wolf became. His temper skyrocketed at the idea of Niall or Alastair anywhere near her. His hands shook, and he actually considered turning around so he could track the boys down and remove them from the picture. His fangs came out, and the craving for blood—

Damon jerked to a stop.

This? Was exactly what he needed to avoid. Those thoughts weren't his; they were his wolf's. The worst day of his life had occurred when the wolf had fully taken charge.

That day had ripped him apart, and he could never face another like it.

He shoved the beast away, this time encouraging his other half to go into hiding. His wolf agreed, slipping away to wherever it was he went at these moments. It was a strange sensation to stand there, still a shifter but mostly human, his senses dulled.

Damon didn't need a spectacular sense of smell to find Addie. She was thirty feet ahead of him, moving rapidly up the hallway, talking to herself as she paused before moving to the next portrait.

"Addie," he called in warning, though he was sure she knew he was there.

She faced him, hands clenched at her sides, her face drawn tight. "He didn't do anything."

"And he'll not do even more in the future," Damon promised.

An instant of confusion rolled over her face as she figured out his twisted phrasing, then she nodded.

"I'm sorry I wasn't there to protect you," he whispered as he closed the distance between them. Guilt rolled in stronger than anything. He should have been there to stop it from happening in the first place.

She shook her head. "You can't be around every minute. And nothing happened. Not really."

"You were scared."

It was clear she was uncomfortable. "You know what? I don't want to talk about it."

He backed off because she was right. It was time for a change of pace. "Come on, I know what you need."

"Whisky shooters?"

"Ha. Maybe later." He held out a hand to her as he

gestured down the hall. "How about some fresh air? I found something you'll like."

She stared at his hand as if it were a live snake, so he let it fall to his side, slightly disappointed.

"Or, instead of a coffee break, I have another suggestion." If he couldn't entice her, he'd pick her up and carry her out, but first he'd try a little more charm. "Ms. Works All The Time And Never Plays, consider this part of your assignment. There are items outside you need to catalog. Hurry up."

He turned without waiting, smiling broadly as her footsteps followed. He moved quickly, his borrowed kilt flapping around his legs—a strange sensation, but one that was growing on him. A few minutes later they'd reached ground level and were outside. Addie increased her pace to catch up with him, striding at his side.

"How did you find out so much about this place already?" she asked.

Damon directed her down one of the side paths, not toward the cottages but toward what he hoped would be a nice surprise. "Went for a run this morning. I never asked. Did you get breakfast?"

"Yes." Addie glanced at him then up ahead where there was a gate in the wall. "Is this the right direction?"

"You betcha." He increased his speed, wanting to see her expression as she walked through the gate for the first time. He rotated as he walked, eyes fixed on her as he paced backward.

The moment she spotted the flowers, her face lit up, and damn if she didn't clap her hands and bounce like an excited kid. "I can't believe I didn't know this was here."

She raced forward to where massive flowerbeds spread in every direction. Gold and crimsons, brilliant purples and delicate pinks were laid out in designs that formed the crest of the Sterling-Wylde clan, as if someone had woven a tartan from the ground itself.

Damon followed her, nodding in agreement every time she discovered something new. He sniffed flowers in appreciation when told to, exclaimed at the amazing layouts, and admired the pruning on the trees.

The entire time he was enchanted with her. All her earlier troubles had vanished, and she was so full of life and light Damon wanted to wrap himself around her and make sure she stayed that way forever.

They'd been outside at least an hour before she whirled on him. "Okay, you're right."

Damon waited. There were lots of things he wanted that to apply to. "Go on."

She moved closer, her smile lighting up as she took a deep breath and glanced around. "I need to take more coffee breaks. It's a crime that I've been here for nearly two weeks, and I hadn't actually come outside."

He let his gaze drop over her in appreciation, far more interested in her than the flowers. "That's why I'm here, baby. I'll keep you safe, even from yourself."

She gave him a wry smile. "It's a terrible habit. Forgetting to stop and smell the roses."

Then damn if she didn't step right into his space, staring up as she slow-motion pressed a hand to his chest. Nervous tension radiated off her in waves, but also hesitant anticipation.

He stayed as still as possible, his wolf tucking in its tail and hiding.

When she let out the breath she'd been holding and didn't jerk back, hope rose in his gut. She stroked him, her fingers tracing his chest muscles before tangling in the cotton laces on his shirtfront. Every inch of him went hard, wanting her soft touch on other, more intimate places.

But then she twirled away, moving toward the gate as she called over her shoulder, "Time for another round of drudgery, I'm afraid."

She seemed totally unaware she'd just jumpstarted one hell of a fantasy. "Fucking in the flowers," he'd call this one. It would make a nice bookend to accompany the "fucking in the shower stall that's big enough for a dozen people, but all I want is her" fantasy he'd also mentally stored away.

"Right. You love your job. Don't try to deny it." Damon ordered his body back to normal as he marched after her, thankful for the kilt. Who knew the extra layers of swingy material would turn out to be the perfect place to hide a boner? "Daily excursions added to the agenda, though, right?"

"Definitely," she agreed. "I did promise to take you for walksies."

He laughed, and they strolled back to the manor in companionable silence, grabbed lunch and returned to the room she'd been working.

Damon settled in his corner, sorting through everything he'd learned so far that day as he watched one petite woman. Inside, a warm glow grew that wanted nothing but her happiness, accompanied by a feverish desire for nothing less than all of her.

6

———

She wasn't ready to sleep. She didn't want to read anymore. What she did want was to do something about the shifter beside her who was driving her mad.

The temperature had dropped, and Damon had started a fire in the fireplace, hauling her couch into position in front of it so they could curl up and enjoy the heat. He'd found a footstool and set it in place to prop his feet on. When she'd teased him to find her one, he'd flashed that cocky grin and patted his lap.

"Put your feet right here, sweetheart."

She shouldn't have. She *wouldn't* have, except the damn man just sat there, goading her with that dangerous sparkle in his summer-sky eyes and the twisted smirk she wanted to kiss right off his lips.

So Addie took the bull by the horns, dropped onto the couch, plopped her feet into his lap and waited in breathless anticipation to see what he'd do next.

Nothing.

Nothing, except rearrange her more comfortably, nod, then return to his reading. Disappointment aside, it still took her a good fifteen minutes before her heart rate dropped to halfway normal.

Damon was working his way through an old book she'd approved for him to bring up from the study. He turned the pages slowly, occasionally humming as if surprised by his discoveries. It was a leather-bound, oversized tome littered with tiny writing in the margins, and every now and then he'd lift the book closer to his nose.

Yup, she was spending more time watching him than reading. Heck, she wasn't even sure what she had opened her ereader to. Addie put it aside and stared into the fire. The itching under her skin returned, as if she was longing for something. To go...somewhere. To do...*something*.

She stared at Damon's strong hands as he cradled the ancient book. No, she'd be honest with herself. After her moment of experimentation in the garden, what she really wanted was his hands on her, caressing her as they—

Knock, knock.

"I'll get it."

Her racing thoughts scattered as she pulled her feet away to allow Damon to leap upright. He placed the book on the side table then hurried across the room to open the heavy door. Confusion drifted over his expression before he leaned his head out and checked both directions.

As far as Addie could tell, the landing at the top of the stairs was empty. "Did we just have a ghost visitor?" she asked, mostly kidding.

Damon's face lit up. He bent over to grab something out of her line of vision. "Maybe. If so, he's one fine fellow and welcome to haunt us at his leisure."

He swung toward her, holding a bottle of golden liquid encased in shimmering crystal.

Addie moved to the edge of the couch. "What? How did that get there?"

The couch dipped beside her as Damon lowered the discovery into her hands. "Don't tell me you've never been visited by spirits before."

She groaned at his bad pun. "Damon…"

"Look, a note." He pulled the paper free from around the bottle's neck, nodding in approval as he read it. "Son of a gun. *Grandmam Susanna insisted you have this. It's from her private collection. Best, Glenn.*"

"Glenn—who's that?" How on earth had Damon made friends so quickly? Friends who were willing to send gorgeous bottles of whisky his way?

Damon headed to the sideboard, answering over his shoulder. "Groundskeeper. Met him this morning. Crossbreed shifter of some sort. He's trustworthy and, depending on the next few minutes, in line to become my new best friend. Him and his grandmother. Awesome woman, your sweetheart of a cook."

He was back an instant later, small drinking glasses in hand.

"You want to pour?" Addie offered.

He shook his head, balanced on his heels in front of her. "You do the honours. It was delivered to your room, after all."

She popped the old-fashioned cork, and a rich, sweet aroma pooled around them. Both she and Damon took deep, appreciative sniffs before she tipped the crystal to the edge of the glass he held.

"Say when."

"You decide. I'm at your mercy," he teased, his voice deep and seductive, and suddenly it was hard to keep the bottle steady.

It was tempting to pour full tumblers, but she resisted, placing the bottle to the side and accepting a glass from Damon. His fingers brushed hers as he pulled away.

He teetered for a moment, catching himself by resting his free hand on her thigh, and sensation hurled its way up her spine. No onslaught of emotion struck, though, and she was curious all over again—did she dare continue?

She'd be a fool not to.

The moment his hand had landed on her thigh, they'd frozen in place like statues. Heat passed from his palm, and it was all she could do to keep her heel planted on the floor, forcing her thigh to remain stationary instead of rubbing against him. Warmth spread from the single point of contact until there were a million tingling threads enveloping her body.

The blue in his eyes deepened, and her wolf nudged upward, wanting to rub all over him.

Wouldn't *that* be the most delightful thing? The dram would fall from her fingers to the floor, consequences ignored as she threw herself into his arms and let him have his wicked wolfie way with her. On the floor, or the couch, heck, maybe the footstool, she didn't care. All of them offered perfect possibilities for playing and pleasure and—

Whoa. She had a wicked imagination, at least.

Damon swallowed hard, his throat moving, and when he spoke his voice was a low, sexy, rumbly tone—one step away from verbal ravishment. "To new friends, and to old friends becoming more intimate ones."

She clicked their glasses together, desperately trying to figure out which she was. A new friend or an old friend, or a new friend of old friends, or—

Thankfully, lifting the glass to her lips jerked her back to reality. Her wolf settled on its haunches and waited for the human side to get over itself. The *more in touch with her animal side* wanted to play with the nice man who was looking at them as if they were a tasty appetizer that was *juuuust* about ready.

Sweet, smooth intoxication slipped over her tongue and down her throat as she stared into two gorgeous blue pools filled with liquid lust. She licked her lips clean of the intoxicating flavour. "That's good whisky," she breathed out, her tongue tangling around the words as if she'd been drinking all night.

No response. None except a slight trembling of his fingers on her thigh in the second before he pulled his hand away. He rocked back on his heels, rising to his feet.

A sense of sadness tore through her system at the loss of his touch as her pulse continued to race out of control.

"That's a *damn fine* whisky." Damon broke his gaze from hers, returning to the bottle and examining the label again. He whistled softly, shaking his head. "I would've suspected Glenn of stealing into the wine cellar and nabbing some old Sterling-Wylde stock, but his grandmam would box his ears if he did such a thing. If this is from her private stash, it seems the old lady has some secrets of her own. Do you know this label?"

He handed her the bottle then settled in the chair to the right of the couch, as if keeping space between them.

Addie ran through her memory banks and found herself in the rare position of lacking information. "I know most of the local brews and whiskies—I did some reading before I came out here, but I don't recognize that label."

"Neither do I." Damon took another sip and pleasure rolled over his expression. "Which tells me it's an exceptionally fine one."

Addie jumped on the change in topic like it was a wayward rabbit. "You know your whiskies, do you?"

His broad shoulders lifted in a modest shrug, shifting under the old linen shirt that fit him oh-so-well and made him oh-so-tantalizing.

It was warm enough he didn't need the tartan draped across his chest but it seemed he liked what he'd found in the suitcases, favouring the blue shades. She had noooooo troubles with that—the colour made his eyes that much brighter, and the lay of the cloth over his...

Damon cleared his throat, and she jerked back, face heating as she realized she'd been staring.

Drooling, you mean, her wolf teased.

Shut up, she snapped in embarrassment, shocked her wolf was being so forward.

She blinked hard to refocus, and Damon was kind enough to ignore her faux pas, going on as if she'd never faltered. "I do have some experience with fine liquors, yes."

"Business or personal?"

"Both."

She hesitated. Curiosity made her want to ask more, but at what point would the questions be rude? He had no reason to explain. He was there as a favour to a friend, giving up his time to ease her fears.

Damon read her mind. "I should've mentioned it earlier, but I was being a bit of an ass. Don't worry, I meant it when I said you're not keeping me from anything. I take assignments like you do, and I'm between jobs. I'm an efficiency checker."

Interesting. "Official, or undercover?"

His grin widened. "You don't know how nice it is to not have to explain what I do. You've probably read all about it."

She'd already mentally shuffled through three or four

different options, but just because she understood what the job might entail, it didn't mean she wasn't interested in his version. "I'd love to hear more, and how it connects with rare, vintage liquor."

Damon poured them both another shot of whisky. "It's not that exciting. Human Resources contact me, usually after there've been financial shenanigans."

"Shenanigans? *Oooh*, the big words are busting out."

"Eloquent, that's me." He raised his glass in the air. "I go in as a new hire, kind of like a *Bosses Undercover* TV show. I can spend up to a month training my way through the system, and at the end of it, I issue a report on where there are gaps, and who's the weakest link. My wolf side helps make the job a little easier. He's pretty adept at finding the loose cogs in an organization, and for the rest, it's a glorified acting job."

She asked a few more questions, and he told her stories, including some high-roller drinking escapades. That led to her sharing about the adventures she'd had while on assignment when she wasn't being stalked by creepy cats. Damon listened as if fascinated, refilling their glasses from time to time,

The fire crackled and the whisky slipped down smoothly, and she felt far more comfortable than she'd imagined possible after such a short time with another person.

She'd started with the wrong impression of him, and the new information made their attraction that much more... attractive. The urge to do something about the simmering heat between them grew hotter the longer it burned.

~

A LULL in the conversation settled in. Comfortable, though, not awkward. They both sat and listened to the fire, her eyes on the flames, his on her.

Because, damn, she was easy to look at. Intriguing, too, in so many ways.

Addie swirled the amber liquid in her glass and sighed mightily. "Well, drat. I feel like a fool."

Damon waited for more clues. Things were going far too well for him to leap in after that kind of comment. He'd be sure to misstep and put them back at square one, and with how skittish she was, he'd hate for that to happen.

Two steps forward, one step back still meant progress.

She met his gaze, a smile on her lips although her lips twisted slightly as if embarrassed. "After hearing about your job... I'd made some assumptions about you, earlier."

Ah. "You thought I was some shiftless jerk."

Her head tipped sharply in acknowledgment, and her smile widened. "You're not at all shiftless."

He laughed. Damn, but he *liked* her. "But I'm still a jerk?"

"What, you won't admit you're a bit of an asshole?"

"One hundred percent asshole. Hundred ten percent if I'm really trying, or when my wolf gets in the way." Damon sniffed his whisky, appreciating the low buzz in his veins caused equally by the high-proof alcohol and his proximity to one very attractive woman. "Although, right now it's just me."

Addie wrinkled her nose in the most adorable manner. "Does that comment have something to do with what happened last night?"

His surprise vanished rapidly as he realized there wasn't much that slipped past her. Of course his momentary panic from last night came to mind. "That's right. You never forget anything."

"I forget lots," she insisted. "I can be as careless and forgetful as the next person. Also, if I work at it, I can replace details in deliberate memories I don't want with other ones. Takes a lot of energy, though, which is why I don't watch a lot of news reports or scary movies."

He stretched out his legs, propping his feet beside her on the couch, toes rubbing her thigh. Deep desire struck again, combined with a unique pleasure. They'd been flirting instead of jumping forward full tilt, in spite of the intense sexual attraction between them.

He was enjoying it. The long game. Going slow.

Another rush of fire lit her eyes as he deliberately stroked her leg.

"Your wolf?" she prompted, her voice fluttering.

Damon took a sip as he considered his words. "We don't get along," he admitted.

Addie sat forward in surprise. "How can you not get along with your wolf?"

He shrugged. "It's been like this since I was a teen. Sometimes things are fine and then others, I don't know how to control him. So I tend to ignore him and keep that part of me under wraps. It's safer."

"Safer isn't always the best," she whispered, causing a low buzz of protective instinct to flare higher. He wanted to make that sad tone in her voice go away. But she lifted her gaze to his again and smiled as what seemed to be a deep-held secret slipped from her lips. "I get how being a shifter isn't all it's cracked up to be at times. My wolf side causes me troubles too," she confessed.

Damon raised a brow.

"Both my parents are Omega wolves, and it's—difficult."

His jaw swung open before he forced his mouth shut. "Well, damn. Talk about rare vintages."

She nodded. "Yeah, yeah, I know. I'm one in a million. Well, not really—there are others like me, but since Omegas are the least common ranking, the odds of two being mates and having a kid is even more *needle in the haystack*."

He'd met maybe three such pairs in all the extensive travels he'd done. Omegas were the heart and soul of a wolf pack, and worked with their Alphas to keep the potentially feral and aggressive members under control. They tended to end up mated to powerful Alphas, not other Omegas.

"And you got something from them, right? Some kind of mind reading? Or the ability to—" *Wait a minute.* He shook a finger at her, more in fun than a real accusation. "You've been cheating and using your supernatural powers to make me behave."

"*Ha.*" Her laugh burst free like a helium balloon shooting skyward to freedom. "If this is you behaving we're in big trouble."

He winked. "You have no idea."

The fire crackled, and he glanced into the flames, tiny fingers of red and gold waving at him. His thoughts remained focused on the petite woman sitting across from him. How she coped with...whatever it was that bothered her. Not knowing what she was suffering through made him twitch. He could fix it, he was *sure* he could.

He needed more information. Damon was just ready to ask when she beat him to the punch.

"Tell me one thing," Addie whispered.

He paused.

She'd linked her fingers together and was twisting them back and forth. "It seems as if there's a connection between us. That's not an Omega, spooky-wooky proclamation, by the way, and maybe I'm wrong, but..." Addie locked eyes with him, golden flecks flashing against the pale brown. "Here we are, two wolves stuck at the end of the universe, or whatever you called it. We're both out of our element. And sometimes—call it what you will, fate or karma—sometimes people get tossed together for a reason."

Every word she spoke drove a blade farther into his core, as if she were a finely trained surgeon cutting straight to the deepest, killing hurt.

Especially when she went on. "Tell me one thing about you that's a secret. Something you wish you could share, but you can't so you hold it deep inside until it feels as if you could explode—"

"My mate died."

He hadn't expected that confession to escape. Neither had she, from the expression of sheer horror rearranging her face. The instant the words left his tongue Damon wished he could take them back, yet there was an enormous relief at having said them.

"Oh, *God*, Damon, I'm so sorry."

Tears pooled in her eyes, and Damon reached up a hand in protest. "It was a long time ago. It's okay. She wasn't... I mean, it's sad, and I hate that she's gone, but we weren't already mated. We were young, and—"

God, he was making a mess of this, yet as he closed the distance between them and settled at Addie's side, he was glad this weird-ass evening had happened. It had been a long time since he'd talked about Caitlin. Not even his best friend knew this story.

Addie caught hold of his arms and gripped tightly. "Go on."

"I had a girlfriend," he shared, "back in my teens. We

started dating when we were thirteen, and nothing got too heavy between us, but I knew Caitlin was the one."

Sorrow shone in Addie's eyes.

Damon shook his head. "We were sure it would happen, but in the meantime it was nice, having a secret that belonged just to us. People knew we liked each other. Heck, we went on a few double dates with my best friend Jim and whoever he was seeing at the time, and he thought we were mostly friends. There'd been none of the struck-by-lightning wolf-connection stuff that happens sometimes. We always figured it would happen when we got old enough, but then—" He swallowed hard. "We got mugged on the way home from a movie."

"Oh, no..." She closed her eyes, body stiffening as if bracing to hear him out. Then she focused again, her wide brown eyes offering him a solid point to cling to as he found the strength to go on.

He couldn't bear to tell it all, so he kept to the general details. Just the facts. "I was full of myself like only a sixteen-year-old alpha-wolf can be, and when the thieves asked for our wallets, I was stupid. I didn't hand everything over. I went after them, instead. Knocked two of them to the ground as quick as a wink, damn near strutting when I turned back to discover the third had run in fear. But in the process, he'd shoved his way past Caitlin and slammed her into the nearest wall. She hit her head hard enough there were complications, and that was it. She was gone."

Addie squeezed harder, her touch centering him. "I'm so sorry."

"If only I hadn't been a cocky bastard."

She took a deep breath. "Oh, Damon, it wasn't your fault. The ones to blame are the bastards who came after you in the first place." Her eyes dipped downward for a moment as if she was reluctant to continue, but she lifted them and met his gaze firmly. "I'm sorry you don't have her in your life. I really want the best for you."

It was the darnedest thing. They weren't simply platitudes she was tossing out—he felt them to his soul. "I know."

He reached up, intending to wipe away the lone tear trickling down her cheek. The one that had escaped as he'd poured out his foolish heart.

She twisted from his touch, and a sharp pain struck his chest. "Addie?"

He looked as if she'd kicked him. Dammit, she *was* a fool. Addie caught hold of him, squeezing his arm over his sleeve, refusing to let him pull away.

"It's not you," she blurted out, scrambling to find the words. "That *difficulty* I mentioned, the one my Omega parents gave me? One skill. One lulu of a talent that made me pull away."

"Go on." Damon waited, far more insecure than she'd seen him to this point. Even when he'd been sharing his deepest pain he'd spoken clearly, but now? He sounded broken.

She took a deep breath. "When I touch people's skin, or they touch mine, I feel what they're feeling. It can be... devastating. And invasive, and I didn't want that to happen to you. That's why I reacted like that."

A deep crease formed between his perfect blue eyes, and she could see him thinking through what her explanation meant.

Waiting for him to respond was torture.

Damon shook his head. "But when I arrived, you kissed me. And in the study, we kissed again."

She'd given that a lot of thought, too. "Both times were a surprise, and that was the most powerful emotion you were experiencing. And I don't mind knowing what you're feeling during a sexual encounter, but it's very intimate. I don't want to overstep my boundaries. I want to touch—"

She broke off, not wanting to admit any more.

If he pulled away, she'd understand. Having someone stroll through your most secret self wasn't an everyday event.

Damon stood and paced a few steps. In spite of appreciating why, she fought to hide her sigh of sadness.

"We slept together," he pointed out.

"Wolf and human. As long as one of us is shifted, there's a barrier in the way."

He laughed softly as he faced her, a hint of a twisted smile on his lips. "Karma's a bitch, right?"

"Sometimes."

He poured them new shots of whisky, carefully handing her the glass without touching her fingers.

"She's also a tricky lady." Damon settled on the couch again, his thigh tight against hers as he leaned back and stretched one arm along the back of the couch. He raised his glass. "No skin, right?"

"Right..." What was he up to?

He tipped back his drink, waiting until she'd done the same before stacking their tumblers together and placing them aside.

Then he laid a hand on her shoulder, tugging her to face him. "You interested in an experiment?"

Heat radiated from where his hand rested, but nothing

untoward happened on an emotional level. "Does it involve wandering the halls searching for cold spots where the damned still cling to the earthly place of their untimely demises?"

Damon grinned. "That's on tomorrow's agenda. Tonight I thought maybe..."

He slid his thumb back and forth, stroking over her shirt. He might as well have used a Taser on her; the electric response of her nerve endings was off the charts.

"You're...touching me."

"Over your clothes." Concern and restrained passion slipped around her like a protective cocoon. "Any negative reactions?"

"Other than my mouth has gone dry and my heart is pumping fast enough to drive a motorboat, no reactions at all," she offered drolly.

He hummed in approval, his gaze following his hand as he trailed his fingers down the front of her T-shirt. Caressing the curve of her breast, slowing as his fingertips slipped over the tight tip of her nipple. "You said there was a connection between us. There's one hell of an attraction, for sure."

Addie groaned as he pinched, arching into his touch as he opened his palm and cupped her. "That feels amazing, but we can't... I mean, I feel guilty."

Damon chuckled as he leaned down and pressed his lips to the upper slope of her breast. "Guilty because we're going to fool around?"

"I can't touch you," she complained. "Except over *your* clothes."

"Maybe, maybe not, but why are you rushing?" Damon slipped off the couch and between her legs, pushing them apart so he could kneel in front of her. "Focus on the experiment. Put your hands on my shoulders and keep them there."

He waited until she'd obeyed, the cool fabric warming rapidly under her fingers from the heat driving off his skin. But that layer, as thin as it was, protected her. A flutter of need rippled through her as he leaned forward, rearranging his hand so the full weight of her breast was cradled in his palm.

Lust-filled eyes met hers as he licked his lips. "I've been dying to do this."

He pressed his tongue to the material, and a wet spot appeared on the beige pyjama top. The sight gave her goose bumps, but more potent was the sensation of moisture. Of heat. They tangled her senses, and desire grew as he closed his lips around her nipple and sucked.

"Oh *Lordy*, that's good."

Addie gave up protesting in favour of wallowing in hedonism. Her head fell back, and she pushed toward him, wanting more. Locking her fingers in place so she didn't interrupt as he nibbled on her through the fabric. Tight coils of pleasure unwound into spirals, connecting her breasts and her core like the ends of a kinky internal Slinky.

After a few passes from side to side, the fabric was wet enough to cling when he lowered his hands to her thighs. His mouth and lips remained in place to torment her with the sweetest of pleasures, while his fingers glided up her legs in precise ovals, each time inching closer to where she was aching to feel him.

So slow, infinitely slow, like the drags of his lips and the touch of his teeth. When he finally brushed his fingers over her sex, it was worth it. Addie squeezed her eyes shut and debated if opening her legs wider and rocking against him would take her to a climax faster, or if it would be wasted energy.

She was already close.

"Eager," Damon teased, his mouth against her breast. Her nipple tingled, and she tugged on his shoulders, trying to get him to return to where she needed him. "I like eager," he murmured as he slowed his pace.

"Don't stop," she begged. "You don't know how long it's been since anyone's fingers but mine have been down there."

"I'm not stopping, just..." He adjusted position, his hand cupping her more firmly as he magically found her clit through the layers and kept rubbing. Only now his groin bumped her shin, and the thick weight of his cock pressed against her as he rocked. A sharp grunt of satisfaction escaped before he returned to driving her mad.

Hands and lips seemed to be everywhere, a relentless assault on her senses as his breathing picked up speed. The edge grew nearer and nearer and—

Sweet release.

The pulse started deep inside and threw her against the couch as his fingers played her like a guitar. The thick cords on his forearms dancing rhythmically as he dragged out her orgasm, snapping his hips faster and faster until he groaned, his free hand clutching her thigh in a vice.

Addie collapsed where she sat, decorum forgotten as she sprawled comfortably, a puddle of satisfaction. Damon rested his head against her chest, his cheek pressed to one wet nipple spot. She stroked his back, patting him happily. "Is that what they call a successful experiment? Because I will totally give you full grades."

"I'll be teacher's pet any time."

Addie laughed. "I had no idea tonight would take this kind of a turn."

Damon pulled away, careful to keep their hands from making contact as he backed away. "I'm glad it did."

"Me too."

He rocked back on his heels. "You're not a virgin, are you?"

She shook her head. "This trick of mine has developed slowly since adolescence. It just got really out of control in the last year."

"And you haven't fooled around since then?"

Addie chuckled at the shock in his eyes. "It's tough to get interested in trying when you're worried. Put it this way. My partner getting distracted during sex was horrible."

"How could someone be distracted with you writhing in pleasure under him?"

Her mouth was dry again. "Whoa, you're good."

Damon grinned.

Still, he needed to know. "Lots of emotions that aren't sexy can happen during sex, especially when *he* spots a spider, and *he's* afraid of them, and suddenly... Well, let's just say most lovers don't like women screaming in their ear in mid-coitus. It interrupts the mood."

He caught her elbow and helped her to her feet. "That would be the wrong sort of exciting."

THE LAST THING he wanted was for her to withdraw, but the last *last* thing he wanted was for her to feel pressured to go faster than she felt safe. Even now she was trembling, her arm under his fingers vibrating, and he didn't think it was aftershocks from the orgasm.

He was good, but not *that* good.

"Let's call it a night. I need a shower first, though."

She hesitated, suddenly shy. "I'd like to try more things."

"Tomorrow," he promised. He leaned over, tempted to kiss her, holding back with every ounce of strength he had. "Sleep in your wolf again. That we know is safe, right?"

Addie nodded, then followed him to the bathroom. "I..." She stood in the doorway, her brown skin flushing as her gaze drifted over him. "Is it too much of a tease if I stay here and watch? When we can't do anything more? Or do you want to do more?"

"Behave." He was tempted, but his thoughts from earlier in the evening echoed. They had a good thing, and going slow wasn't a bother. In fact, it added something to their relationship. Something he'd not had since he'd lost Caitlin.

Addie might not be his mate, but she was special, and for more reasons than her Omega background. He deliberately kept space between them, reaching over his shoulders to catch hold of his shirt and pull it over his head. He bunched the fabric into a ball and tossed it to the floor in front of him.

"No touching. That's my rule. You can look all you want."

Addie leaned on the doorframe, her pyjama pants and still-damp sleep shirt a thin barrier between them, and suddenly he wanted that gone as well.

"I charge a toll for the ladies to ogle me while I shower." He smirked, playing with the button on his kilt.

"A toll?" Addie straightened, mischief on her face as well. "I have no idea what you could possibly ask for in payment." She twisted the hem of her shirt between her fingers and, holy shit, he was a stupid fool because he might have just come in a very schoolboy fashion, but his dick was hard again.

"Take it off, sweetheart. Let me see." She shimmied the fabric upward, and he watched intently as her belly button, then her ribs, and then those perfect brown nipples he'd been sucking on earlier, albeit through the shirt, came into view. "Holy fuck, I'm going to drop dead," he warned.

It was like eating a smorgasbord in reverse. He already knew what sounds she made when she came. Already knew how she would tremble under his touch, how she tightened ever so slightly in that instant before climax.

Now he got to see the treasures he'd been fondling only moments earlier.

"Drop your trousers," he commanded.

"Kilt first," Addie insisted, slipping a hand under her pyjama pants.

Damon's brain went off-line. Naked from the waist up, her pants hid what she was doing from his sight, but he could imagine what was happening. The soft fabric moved the lightest bit as her knuckles showed against the worn cotton. "If you make yourself come, I'm really going to die. Right here, right now."

"Ditch the kilt, Damon," she ordered, easing her shoulders against the wall. Her lower lip slipped between her teeth, and she hummed softly, her fingers moving again in an intriguing manner.

"*Damn...*"

A moment later the kilt was on the ground, and Damon stood stark naked in his socks, all of him hard and aching, his cock pointing straight at her as if she were the North Pole and he were a compass.

She worried that lower lip a little more before breathing

out a happy sigh. "Looking at you is like wandering through the Louvre in Paris and coming across one of Michelangelo's finest works. Are you sure your name isn't David?"

"You're flustered." He gripped his cock tighter and stroked a few times because it was impossible not to. "David is in Florence, sweetheart. Not Paris."

Her eyes were focused on his hand. "See, I do forget things," she said. "I should let you shower."

She pretended to get ready to leave.

"You move one inch toward that door, and I will wrap you in a blanket, take you to the top of the highest tower and give you so many screaming orgasms the boys will think they have a sex-maniac ghost haunting the place."

Addie snickered. "That doesn't sound like much of a threat..."

But she hooked her thumbs under the edge of her pyjama pants and wiggled out of them, her breasts dipping as she pushed the fabric to her ankles. She kicked the material aside, and it joined the pile of his things on the ground.

She stood, one leg flexed, weight resting with a hip jutting out, her hands dangling at her sides. Like a statue in the museum she'd mentioned, but so much better. Not cold, white marble, but warm, brown skin that begged to be touched.

Somehow, he was going to find a way to make that happen.

They stared at each other, and then she blew him a kiss and shifted, turning into her wolf form with a shimmer. Light pulsed, the magic taking her from beautiful creature to beautiful creature, and Damon was pretty sure he could fall in love with either one of them.

Addie padded back into the bedroom as Damon rinsed off quickly, no longer wanting to prolong the time before he could be with her.

When he got to the bed, Addie had already curled up with her nose tucked under her paws, soft and relaxed. Damon took full advantage and wrapped himself around her, guarding her with his body.

No one who wasn't a shifter could understand how natural it was for them to be naked and touch, and no one who wasn't a shifter could understand how much she must have hurt, dealing with limited touch over the past year.

She deserved a little TLC.

Cradling her all night long was no hardship. Neither was waking up in time to be out of bed and dressed before her, speeding down to the kitchen to offer Grandmam Susanna a kiss before raiding the cupboards, looking for breakfast.

The old woman flushed, shaking her head as he thanked her for the treat she'd sent their way the night before. "It was doing me no good sitting on the shelf," she said, slapping his fingers away from the sausage patties frying briskly in the pan. "I have trays for you and the nice young lady nearly ready. Wait a little, my lad. There's no use rushing good things."

Her words echoed the thoughts he'd had the night before.

He took the stairs two at a time, balancing the tray easily in his hands as he carried up two full plates of food and a steaming carafe of coffee for them to enjoy out on the balcony in the morning sunshine.

Other than nearly tripping over another house cat at the top of the stairs, the day continued in a most spectacular way. The coffee was perfect, their breakfast conversation general enough to be safe and yet entertaining. The best part was watching pleasure bloom on Addie's face as she bit into a sausage. Damon had to jerk his gaze away to stop from staring at her lips.

She finally patted her napkin against her mouth and pushed aside her empty plate with a satisfied sigh. "We're switching rooms today," she announced. "This time you get to do some work."

Damon struck a muscle pose, offering his biceps for admiration.

"Yes, I see you. There's nothing wrong with your beefcake," she agreed with a smirk.

"I'll lift and tote," he said, "but you have to agree I'm in charge of our breaks and quitting time." She loosened the band of her watch and held it out. Damon accepted it before another thought struck. "You don't have a clock in your head as well, do you?"

Addie laughed. "One weird talent is enough, thank you."

Then she led him into what had to be a storage room, walls lined with unlabeled boxes all covered in heavy layers of dust.

He got to lift then. He got to do *lots* of lifting. By the time she'd gone through a dozen of the boxes, he was covered with an inch of dust.

He was about to suggest time for their first break when she gave a low whistle, holding up a linen paper tied together with a length of a fine lace. "Lookee here," she said. "The plot thickens, Watson."

Damon leaned on the table beside her. "A little deducting from that comment makes me think you've discovered another will."

"Possibly. I'm going to open it with you as an

eyewitness, if you don't mind. I don't want to make a fuss if it's a bunch of old love letters, but this is the type of paper Lord Sterling-Wylde used for the other wills."

Damon settled his arm against hers for reassurance, and she glanced up, quickly offering a smile before turning back to the task of untying the delicate string.

Addie carefully unfolded the first part, and that seemed enough to confirm her suspicions. "*Final testament of Lachlan Sterling-Wylde.* We have will number five. The boys are not going to be happy."

She didn't open it any further, instead folding it carefully and placing it aside out of the dusty area where she'd been working.

"You're not curious what it says?"

"Of course I'm curious, but it's not my business. I can wait until the official word comes out. And luckily, the executor is dropping by today for his weekly update from me. I can give this to him without mentioning it to the boys."

"If they give you any trouble, I'm here for you," he reminded her.

Addie nodded. "You are, and thank you for that." She paused, staring past him at the box in the far end of the room, shaking her head. "Someone must have hit a sale on leather journals. I swear I've seen a dozen of those golden-toned covers. I keep finding them all over, in places that make no sense."

"You're just annoyed you can't work methodically," he teased lightly. "*Books belong in the library.*"

She stuck out her tongue, and Damon couldn't resist. He leaned forward and planted a kiss against her lips, slipping his tongue against hers for a brief instant before pulling away. Watching carefully for her reaction.

Her eyes widened and a pulse beat a million miles an hour at the base of her throat, but she didn't start screaming or anything, so that was good.

"Is this another experiment?" she whispered.

Oh hell, no. Damon trapped her in place, one hand on either side of her hips at the table. "Definitely not. This is our break time. Ready to get refreshed?"

A flash of nervousness passed her eyes. "What if…"

"Then we stop."

He didn't bother to discuss it any further. Just leaned forward, closing the distance between them. Her gaze was fixed on his lips, hers parting slightly, warm breath wafting past his cheek.

The other times they'd kissed it had been in a wild rush —she was right that surprise had been the foremost emotion. But now he wanted something different. Anticipation. Sensual longing.

He leaned into her, their torsos brushing, completely safe with their clothing as a barrier. The heat of her body and his meshed together as he lowered his head.

Addie tilted her head back and to the side, sucking in a quick gasp before he made contact. Soft lips met his, warm and enticing. He offered a kiss then slipped back half an inch, coming forward to repeat the motion a dozen times. It gave her time to react if needed, time for him to pull away, but the only thing she did was press tighter against him, hungrily returning his advances.

Damon took a chance and slid his hand up her back until he was cradling her head, angling her to the side so he could kiss her deeper. Their tongues slipped against each other, tentative touches that sent thrills through his entire body, urgent need rising that he tucked aside as he enjoyed the simple pleasure of this contract.

The slightest whisper of a negative response and he'd retreat to the other side of the room faster than a lightning bolt, but the only sounds from her were moans of happiness. Pleasure. *Need*.

He could have kept going for a hell of a lot longer, but instead he pulled back, breathing heavily as they stared into each other's eyes.

"I have no idea how you did that," Addie whispered, utter amazement in her tone. "Nothing. I mean, nothing other than I want another helping, please."

"Such a greedy girl. I have to keep my eye on you. Who knows what mischief you get up to all by yourself in these dark lonely rooms?"

"Ha. If there's any mischief you'd want to be involved."

Damon played the innocent. "Me? *Involved* in mischief? I think the word you're looking for is instigator."

She laughed softly, a flirty smile tugging her lips. "Scoundrel."

"You like scoundrels." He reluctantly let her go.

It was the strangest thing—his wolf was completely MIA, and had been since the previous day, but he wasn't worried anymore. Now he was focused on Addie and what they could get up to during the next break. Something to keep testing the waters, especially if it dragged out the sexual tension between them.

He loved a good challenge, and this was one of the most pleasurable he'd had in a long time.

8

———

*A*ddie finally knew why Damon was there—to torment her.

She'd thought Lillie had sent him to help, but it had actually been a declaration of war by her best friend. He kept the Sterling-Wylde boys at bay while simultaneously driving her completely and utterly mad.

Three days. Three devastatingly wonderful and *frustrating* days.

That's how long had passed since their intimate discussion that night in front of the fire. Three days where they'd shared kisses and brief caresses, Damon sneaking up on her while she worked, and brushing past her at every opportunity.

At no time did any wild rush of emotion overwhelm her, at least not from him. Her libido was doing a great job sending her blood pressure skyrocketing all on its own.

He'd gotten her off on the bed last night. Made her strip before ordering her to lie flat out on the soft linen covering the mattress. She'd been sure they were actually going to have sex, but instead he'd taken the silky soft top sheet and laid it over her, caressing her through the material as he kissed her senseless.

Orgasms were wonderful things, but she really wanted sex. And she wanted to touch him, which hadn't been part of the agenda, no matter how much she tried. He had all those muscles she'd gotten to look at, that her fingers ached to explore. Yet Damon was the master of distraction, always finding a way to stay out of reach and turn the sensual exploration in her direction.

It was hard to pout when she was shaking from yet another climax.

To top it all off, her wolf was sulking. They hadn't had a whiff of Damon's shifter side, which all things considered was really weird.

Enough. Today she was going to do something about their stalemate. Because as much fun as they were having, and how much better her job was going with Damon's protective presence, Addie wanted more. She wanted to *give* more, and this time he would damn well accept it.

Choosing the right moment was more difficult than deciding it was going to happen. Pouring rain kept them inside all morning, but after lunch, the sun burst free.

"Break time," Damon announced, rising from the chair where he'd been quietly keeping an eye on her.

"Outside?" Addie suggested.

He nodded. "Garden, or down by the lake?"

Hmmm. Wide open spaces, or plenty of hidden nooks and spaces for a secret rendezvous? "Garden."

In spite of her secret agenda they wandered for over an hour first, talking about their families. Finding out what he'd done for fun growing up in New York City pointed out how very different his life had been from what she'd experienced in rural Scotland.

They didn't have a lot in common, and yet she couldn't deny the attraction. And after the fooling around they'd done, she was pretty sure going all the way wouldn't be a problem for her *woo-woo* talent thingie.

Even if it was—she wanted to risk it.

They strolled side-by-side, Damon flirting outrageously, and the ball of heat in her core continued to expand.

It had to be okay to do more. She wanted it to be okay.

"I have something to show you," he murmured. He'd snuck up behind her and briefly enveloped her in his arms, nuzzling at her neck affectionately for a split second before whirling away.

"You're being awfully forward."

Mischief danced in his eyes as he straightened, sturdy wall that he was. His muscular body was relaxed but alert, and she took a moment to appreciate every solid inch of him. He was built like the finest of wolves. Strong muscles, not bulky, but enough she wanted so much to run her fingers over him, stroking his smooth, marble-like surfaces. Smooth but for the dusting of hair at the center of his chest and the line that led from his belly button down into his kilt...

And why on earth had he pulled off his shirt again? Her legs didn't seem very stable all of a sudden.

"I've already seen this." The shaky *oh my God* instant lust that hit her came out sounding slightly sarcastic.

Damon flashed a wicked smile. "Behind this wall is the next thing we're going to do for a break."

"And it involves taking off our clothes?"

Oh boy. That wasn't the question she should've asked, not only because it sent him prowling toward her, but because everything in her was jumping up and down with delight, instantly wanting to strip. "I should get back to work," she teased.

He moved within touching distance, stroking her arm as he looked her over from top to bottom. "Tell me you don't know everything you just saw, from the sundials to the medallions in the grass. You'll add it to the inventory, right?"

"So I'm not really goofing off. I'm working."

Damon nodded. "You need to do a thorough search"—he jerked a thumb behind him—"including what's in there. I've already checked it out, so I know exactly where we need to end up. Tag. You're it."

He whirled away before she could protest, disappearing behind a heavy wooden door he left propped open. Addie laughed out loud, the noise echoing happily off the stone walls.

Perfect. Oh, so perfect. Damon had played right into her hands.

She peeked around the corner to make sure the coast was clear. Then she stepped into a small alcove, stripped off her clothing and piled it neatly on the nearby bench.

Addie shifted, embracing the wolf side of her. She needed to track her quarry, and this was the best way. The sweet sensation of changing left her more ready to find him, shaking her fur into place before sniffing the air. The normal scents of wilderness greeted her, like the small animals that lived nearby, and the songbirds going off in the nearby tangled rosebushes.

And Damon's scent, wild and intoxicating. Hunger of a specific kind took hold, and Addie pushed aside everything else and let her wolf take charge.

She raced through the doorway, refusing to be distracted by the scents left by passing rabbits and stray raccoons. Damon had twisted and turned around bushes that rose higher and higher over her head, and she realized they'd entered the labyrinth.

Every step she took revealed new secrets hidden in small alcoves notched into the living walls of the maze. They would've been set up as markers for humans wandering through, but she didn't need them. She had Damon's scent clanging through her head, a rich, sensual aphrodisiac.

Addie sped up. Racing toward him as if being pulled by a magnet.

Her wolf functioned on a more basic level, and while there were times she disliked its straightforward thinking, there was nothing wrong with what was currently on the beast's mind.

Craving, lust, a desire for satisfaction.

A desire to *play*. Damon would not only rock her socks off, he'd put a smile on her face while he did so.

The touching they'd shared over the past couple days gave enough reassurance she wasn't about to step off a cliff into dangerous emotional feedback. How he was controlling it, she had no idea, but the only thing she'd ever felt when they touched was desire, not pain.

She wanted to give in return.

Addie rounded the corner so fast her hind legs skidded on the path. He'd made his way to the center of the labyrinth. Ahead, a low concrete bench surrounded a fountain that shot water skyward, droplets shining like liquid sunshine as they fell with a splash into the pristine pool.

All that was taken in with her wolf senses. The human side was focused on the blond god standing to one side, hands resting on his lean hips as he smiled in her direction.

No holding back, no need to resist.

Maybe she was making a huge mistake, but she'd find out soon enough. She ran straight at him, muscles bunching as she accelerated to full speed. One final crouch then she leapt, changing to her human form in midair.

❧

DAMON MOVED INSTINCTIVELY to catch her, twirling as momentum brought her upper torso in full contact with his. He'd barely had time to peek at the small, perfect curves of her breasts, with tiny brown nipples that were now pressed against him.

He'd been holding back and taking it slow, but secretly, he'd hoped this would happen. Having her naked in his arms was the most perfect thing he'd ever experienced.

"You found me," he teased, bringing her to the edge of the fountain. He sat on the wide concrete bench, draping her over his lap as he cupped her chin in his fingers.

"It's a treasure hunt. I expect a reward." Sheer delight in her tone.

He could work with that. For now he took what she offered, holding her face steady as he leaned in to connect their lips. A wave of sensation rolled over him, and he warned his wolf to stay in hiding as his excitement built. "Tell me. The instant you need to, tell me and I'll stop."

"We're fine. We're…oh, *yes*, this feels so *good*…"

She moved against him, undulating in place so their naked torsos rubbed together as he took control of her lips.

Damon slipped his free hand around her, spreading his fingers wide over her lower back and locking her in place. The heat of her sex centered firmly over the wrought-iron shaft behind his kilt.

God, he loved the Scots.

All it would take was two moves and he could be inside her. One to push away the fabric, and the second to slam her hips down as he thrust up, and he wanted that so badly, but first...

He lifted her. Hands wrapped around her hips as he hoisted her in the air and stood her on the bench beside him. She ran her fingers through his hair, a secretive smile folding her lips.

Damon twisted on the bench and caught hold of her butt, squeezing his fingers into the soft surface as he pulled her close enough to press a kiss to her belly button. "That was a very good bit of tracking. You have a lovely wolf."

"Thank you. I like her too." She petted him again. "I'd like to meet your wolf, as well."

He didn't want to be distracted. "Right now I have other things on my mind."

It was the first time he got to touch her breasts without anything between them. He thought he'd enjoyed himself before, but the sensation of his tongue against her soft skin— sublime. He teased and tasted, nipping before closing his lips around the tight points and sucking.

An extraordinary variety of sounds escaped her lips as he drifted a hand down her body, slipping a finger gently through her folds. Wetness greeted him, and he brought some up to slowly circle her clit until she was squirming.

Suddenly he was the prey instead of the predator, Addie dropping to her knees on the grass in front of him.

She looked up, eyes sparkling, running her hands down his thighs and over the kilt until she connected with his knees. "You've really embraced the Scottish tradition, haven't you?"

Under her fingers his kilt bunched together as she bared

more of his legs, inching the fabric toward his groin. "Are you asking what you'll find under my kilt?"

"Oh, I already know what I'll find. Something tasty..."

He totally cheated. He ignored the button and the buttonhole and simply ripped back the tartan aside to leave himself naked and at her mercy.

Addie's eyes widened as she slipped her hand up and caught hold of the root of his cock. "For *me*?"

"All for you."

He clamped his teeth together to stop from shouting in surprise. He'd expected her to go slow. She was supposed to tease him the way he'd been teasing her for days, but she seemed to have an entirely different agenda. Addie lifted the head of his cock, aimed it at her mouth and then damn near swallowed him whole.

Damon leaned back and clenched the edge of the concrete bench, his fingers tightening on the solid surface as wet heat enveloped him. Her mouth was heaven around him, and when she pulled back, applying wicked suction, he saw stars.

She was full of surprises. Instead of moving over him in a steady rhythm, she wrapped her fist around the base of his cock and jacked him hard while using her mouth and lips on the sensitive head. Stroking with her tongue before drawing in rhythmic pulses. Every touch an assault on his senses that gave him nowhere to go except straight into a boiling cauldron of need.

Somehow he cracked open one eye to check she wasn't continuing on in spite of being in pain.

Nope. Addie noticed his gaze and tossed him a wink, increasing her speed another notch until he was one second away from losing control.

He reached down and pulled her off, desperate to take the next step.

Addie pouted. "I wasn't done with that."

"I need to use it," he panted, laying her out on the concrete platform, his kilt spread to protect her from the hard surface.

Beside them the fountain provided a serenade, the falling droplets striking the water's surface like tiny bells while small gusts of wind covered them with a fine mist. She caught hold of his shoulders and attempted to pull him on top.

He shook his head. "My turn."

The past couple days had been a salute to his creativity, finding ways to have a sexual relationship without actually touching, skin on skin. He'd enjoyed himself—listening to Addie climax was addictive. Only he'd gotten to touch but never taste her, and he was about to correct that.

Damon dropped his head between her thighs and put his mouth on her sex, slipping his tongue through her folds and taking a deep lick.

Oh, hell, *yes*. It was worth the wait.

"I might be here a while," he warned.

Addie laughed, the sound turning into a groan of pleasure as he found her clit and teased it with the tip of his tongue. "Poor, tortured me," she complained.

He took his time, lapping up her sweetness, stroking too gently to set her off. Slipping his fingers into her and teasing her until she was quaking, her hips rattling in time with his slow thrusts.

When he finally put his lips around her clit and sucked, she called his name and came, core tightening around him—a precursor of what he had to look forward to.

Damon rose over her before changing his mind, turning

her relaxed body in his arms and settling her in his lap the way they'd started. Only now, *hallelujah*, his kilt was gone and her wet core was right against his cock.

Addie rose and fell in a leisurely fashion, gripping his shoulders as she offered him a satisfied smile. Damon gritted his teeth and held back as she played, her fingers dancing in the hair at the back of his neck as the heat of her sex danced against his aching length. Teasing. Taunting. Getting him wet, but no farther.

"This is fun," she whispered. "I like touching you. Feeling you against me. I loved your fingers inside me."

"Time for my cock," he demanded. "I want to feel you around me, all wet and needy."

He lifted her hips and helped position her, then he slipped his hands up to cup her breasts as he stared into her eyes and let her take control.

SHE'D GUESSED RIGHT ABOUT so many things, but the most important was—oh, my *goodness*, he was built like a tank. *Everywhere*. Addie pushed down another fraction of an inch, savouring the slow stretch as his thick cock filled her a little more with every motion.

She was wet, not just from the climax, but from sheer anticipation. Sheer *appreciation* for the drool-worthy man in front of her. When her butt finally landed all the way in his lap, she wiggled forward, rubbing her clit against him, and sighed happily.

He caught her chin. "Everything good?"

She double-checked, but the entire time she'd had nothing but her own emotions whipping though her system. "We're great. Honest."

He nodded, then that look of mischief flashed in his eyes. "I hope you don't think you get to be in control the entire time?"

"Hardly. But I do get to do this whenever I want." She tightened her internal muscles, clamping down hard on his cock and smiling in satisfaction as his eyes rolled back in his head.

He snapped to attention, evil anticipation shining out. "That's mean. Do it again."

As if in retaliation, he thrust a hand between them and found her clit, placing his thumb over it and giving a hard pinch.

A shot of sheer pleasure raced through her. She squeezed.

He rubbed harder.

Addie pumped herself on him, using him like a dancing pole. Damon picked up the rhythm, rocking his hips upward until both of them were a split-second away from coming. And then no longer a split second, but roaring through the moment.

She closed her eyes and let the wave of pleasure drench her. Intimate contact without overwhelming pain was a gift beyond measure.

Her pussy pulsed around him, squeezing so tightly it dragged another gasp from him along with her name as he lost control. The fingers of his left hand pressed hard into her hip, and she wondered if she'd be bruised. She didn't mind one bit, not as aftershocks rocked her over and over.

Seconds later...

Minutes?

She had no idea. They sat there, tangled together, until their breathing returned to normal. He stroked her cheek, and she caressed his shoulders, determined to stay where she was as long as possible. Bodies connected, warmth passing between them like an erotic heater.

"That was fun," Damon breathed out.

"I had a wonderful time," she confessed.

"And no troubles?"

"None." She didn't want to analyze why. The only thing she wanted?

Was to do it again.

9

———

*A*ddie reached into the air, stretching hard to loosen some of the kinks in her body.

Instantly Damon was there, his firm hands working the knots out of her neck and shoulders, thumbs digging in just the right amount until her brain turned to mush.

"You shouldn't do that to me," she complained.

"Do what?" His hands slipped down her arms until they settled on her hips. He moved in closer, tucking his face against her neck as he breathed in deep then licked her skin.

A shiver ran over her and she wiggled free, laughing as she turned. "Distracting man."

"Delicious woman," Damon returned. "Fine. I'll be good. For now."

After giving her a wink that promised more later, he sat at the dining table and pulled out his phone to play a game.

She went back to work on the china cabinet tucked in the corner of the room, glancing every now and then at him, a smile on her lips the entire time.

No, this wasn't how she usually spent her days at work, but she wasn't about to complain. Not about the extracurricular activity they were getting to enjoy, or about how his presence made her feel so safe.

The Sterling-Wylde boys continued to slip in and out of her peripheral vision, but for the most part they stayed out of the way. There were no more secret-peek-hole occurrences—Damon had warned her about the possibility, and they'd made sure to identify them in each new room she worked. Alastair had tried to make nice a couple of times, but Damon stood at the ready like an avenging warrior, ready to defend her at the slightest wrong move.

Alastair took it as a challenge, talking for at least five minutes before giving Damon a final defiant glare then drifting away.

Niall had been scarcer. She wasn't sure what Damon had said to him that day in the library, but he seemed to have taken it to heart. The most she saw was the rare glimpse of him stomping through the hallways, the tails of his long cloak swaying as if he were hurrying off to a banquet at Hogwarts.

Only his scent was often in the room when she came in to begin work. She didn't bother to tell Damon because he had just as good a sniffer as she did, but it bothered her, and made her doubly grateful for his presence.

"Ten minutes until our break," Damon reminded her. His eyes flashed with the promise of another limb-shaking, satisfying excursion.

"Thank you." The words burst out.

He tilted his head in question at her out-of-the-blue reaction.

"I feel safe because you're here. I want you to know how much I appreciate that."

He stayed where he was, leaning back his chair and propping his feet on the edge of the antique table. "I should be a gentleman and tell you it's no problem, but maybe there's a bill to be paid."

Damon wiggled his brows like some comic-book villain, and she giggled. "You also have a terrific sense of humour. I like that about you."

"Who said I was joking?"

Addie hesitated. He had to be joking. "You're not about to charge me bodyguard hours."

He leaned forward, the feet of the chair coming to rest with a solid clunk as his elbows hit the table. He admired her hungrily as if she were the main course at a dinner banquet. "You'll find my bill is as creative as I am."

"Whatever it takes to get the job done." Addie shivered from the intensity of his stare.

"Don't talk about 'jobs' right now."

It took a second for her to figure out his meaning, then she couldn't resist answering in kind, dangerously poking her favourite wolf.

"I wouldn't want to *blow* my chances." She breathed out the words before moaning as if she were on the edge of an orgasm.

He growled. "Get back to work, woman, so I don't feel guilty about ravishing you later."

A polite knock sounded at the door, and Alastair appeared, peeking his head around the corner. He smiled at Addie before tensing as soon as he realized Damon was glowering at him.

"Ahh, there you are." He motioned with a finger crook. "I require your services, my good man. Out in the yard."

Damon rose slowly, suspicion on his face. "I'm supposed to help Addie."

"You're supposed to do heavy lifting," Alastair

corrected. He glanced around the room. "Anything you need help with in the next while?"

Addie could lie, but there was nothing in the room too big for her to deal with herself. She shook her head, smiling reassuringly at Damon. "Go on. I'll need you later, though, in the library. If that's okay?"

Damon nodded his agreement, turning to Alastair. "I'll catch up with you in a moment." He waited until Alastair was gone before coming to her side. "If you don't want me to go..."

"Don't be silly. I'm fine. Niall is not going to show up again. I think you tied his tail in a good, solid knot the last time he bothered me."

"Hmm, I didn't, but that's a great idea if we ever need it in the future."

She gave his arm a squeeze. "I look forward to our coffee break this afternoon, whatever time you *blow* back into the room."

Suggestion hung on the air between them.

"Between now and then you should lose your panties," he growled.

Oh lordy. Her heart skipped a beat and said panties got instantly wet. "Well now. Do ladies do such things?"

"Sauce for the goose..." A low rumble escaped his chest, and he leaned in to kiss her. A firm and possessive touch that sent her senses reeling before he strolled from the room, casting a cocky glance over his shoulder as he winked farewell.

Addie finished her work in the dining hall far sooner than expected. She made her way to the second floor, pausing to peer out the window. Damon was working with a group of the local men, moving antique buggies around the yard. Full sun lit the area, and he'd stripped to the blue kilt around his hips. The firm muscles in his chest and upper body corded as he put hands to one of the old carts and pushed. It crept across the yard, two other men directing at the front. *Lordy.* He was strong as a workhorse, and all those muscles were hers every time he focused his attention on her.

And...she was drooling.

Addie wiped her mouth and headed to her next work area. She'd been cataloging her way through the library one section at a time. It was the biggest room in the entire house, with the most work, and contrary to Damon's tease about working methodically, she'd found in the past it was best to break up the most detailed tasks.

She walked to the middle of the room, pausing to admire her surroundings. This was another reason why she loved her job. Cataloging history was one thing, but books were an adventure all in themselves. And old libraries had the best of both worlds—beauty and history, tangled together.

The shelves here were two storeys high, the second level accessed by spiral staircase in the corner. The lower shelves were reached by sliding ladders, their curved upper edges attached to a smooth, metal railing running the perimeter of the room.

She glanced around in appreciation then headed to where she had stopped the previous week except...*shoot.*

"Arghhhhh," she shouted into the quiet of the library. "My iPad."

Like she'd informed Damon days earlier, having an eidetic memory didn't mean she never pulled stupid boners. She marched back to the door, intending to grab her iPad from the bathroom where she clearly remembered leaving it beside the sink.

The knob turned, but the door remained stubbornly shut. Tugging harder changed nothing, and after trying a dozen different things, including throwing her weight at it, she gave up.

Stupid old doors, in silly old buildings. At least she'd told Damon where she would be, so once he was done, he'd come to get her.

Addie returned to the window and glanced out. Sure enough, he was still there, and she watched for while, ogling him happily before turning back to her task. She'd just have to take notes on paper and transfer to her files later.

She started at the bottom with a set of reference material for gardening, getting absorbed in her task for an hour. She pushed the ladder aside to access the collection better, but it caught on something, and she glanced up in surprise.

A section of books in the top row seemed oddly out of place. Most of the antique covers were grouped together, but here a batch had gold spines instead of brown, and one of them was sticking out far enough to get in her way.

Addie had one foot on the second rung when the door creaked opened behind her. She whirled, calling out in a panic, "Don't shut it."

ADDIE'S SHOUT of concern caught him off-guard. He hadn't sensed anything, and for one moment, absolute fear shot through him, and his wolf broke to the surface for the first time in days. Damon shoved the beast away as fast as he'd risen. "What's wrong?"

"The door locked on me. Check it before you close it, or we'll be trapped in here all night."

His heart rate dropped in relief. The door—that was nothing scary. He examined it carefully, working the tumblers a few times before shutting himself outside and then in. "Not sure what I did but the problem is solved."

Addie offered a smile that sent flames through his body. "My hero."

Hallelujah. Exactly what he wanted to hear. After spending a couple hours in hard physical labour, he was ready for a different kind of exercise.

He'd been annoyed at Alastair at first, but the job had turned out to be a real one, and Glenn and the other men of the manor were easy to work with. In all, Damon felt it had been a good use of his time, joking and getting to know the locals—solid individuals, the lot of them.

The fact Alastair stayed, probably intent on mocking him for being a lowly labourer, didn't bother Damon one bit. It meant the man wasn't annoying Addie. And Niall had remained in sight as well, going over the carriages as they moved them as if worried another will would miraculously appear at any moment.

Yup, with Addie safe, Damon didn't care how many times he got hooked to a cart and used like an old horse.

But now? Now he had something else on his mind, and so did she, from the expression on her face and the way she was coquettishly tiptoeing her way around the room.

Locking the door from the inside.

Oh, hell *yeah.*

"Your rescuer requires attention," he warned.

She clasped her hands together like an old-time maiden facing an evil villain. "Oh, dear, is my virtue in danger?"

Damon stalked toward her, the urgency in his gut riding higher the longer they were together. She was exactly what he looked for in a playmate, exactly what he liked as a lover.

Eager and willing. And hotter than a Fourth of July firecracker. "Virtuous women. Do you know what I do to such ladies?"

She'd made it back to her starting point, shimmying up the first rungs of the ladder to gaze down at him, delight dancing in her eyes as he took hold of either side of the ladder, his hands firmly trapping her hips. "You do dastardly things to them? I hope."

"I do fucking dirty things to them. Dirty, nasty, *wonderful* fucking things." He caught hold of her skirt and shoved it to her waist in one move. "Hmmm. I told you no panties, sweetheart."

He glanced up, her big eyes washing him with desire as the flecks of whisky gold sparkled. "I must have forgotten."

Damon chuckled. "You never forget anything," he reminded her.

"Not true. I never forget anything for long, but I do forget things." The last words came out in a gasp as he stroked his fingers along her inner thigh. He dragged his gaze off her face, watching his hands instead as he snuck one finger under the edge of her pale pink panties and drew them down her leg.

"Hold tight to the ladder," he ordered. "Don't let go."

He made sure her right foot was solidly on the rung then caught hold of her left leg, resting her knee on his shoulder. The position put her wide open to him, the scent of her desire growing, and he was ready in an instant.

"I'm going to fuck you with my tongue," he told her happily, as if he had just ordered a coffee at his favourite coffee shop. "And after you've come a few times, I'll fuck you with my fingers."

He leaned forward and pressed a kiss to her mound. Addie moaned, keeping her hands where he'd told her, which was good because he didn't want to worry about her falling. Hell, if she did fall, it would be into him, but he wanted her focused on the pleasure he was about to give her.

And then he didn't have the willpower to wait any longer. He shoved forward and licked her top to bottom eagerly, as if he'd gone without a drink for days. He licked and sucked, wrapping his lips around her clit and pulsing rhythmically until she rocked against him, echoing every move he made. He worked harder, flicking his tongue until she shook, a gentle orgasm this time, which was fine, because this was just a warm-up.

He pulled back, his mouth wet from her body. He reached up a hand and drew his fingers over her lips. "Open for me, pretty wolf. Get my fingers wet. As wet as you are, so I can fuck you with them. I'm gonna make you scream, and after that we'll see about what else I put in this pretty cunt of yours."

Her eyes widened, her mouth opened in surprise at his crude words, and he took total advantage, slipping his fingers in over her tongue. Pulsing them slowly until they were soaking wet.

"Was that too dirty for you, my Scottish princess?"

Her eyes were still wide, but she shook her head as he thrust his fingers into her mouth, preparing them for what he was about to do next.

"Hmmm. I'm not a hero, I'm one of your neighboring clansmen, come to ravage my enemy. And you are my plunder. My reward, and I'm going to spoil you, and you'll be mine, forever." He pulled his fingers from her mouth with a *pop*, expecting her to laugh, or expecting her to tell him to get on with the fucking.

Instead, she batted her lashes. "Please, Laird Wolf. I

accept your rule. My husband was a despot, and you have done me a favour by ridding him of his foul life. Take your reward." She licked her lips, staring down intently, and between one second and the next the room was far too hot.

It was a good thing all he was wearing was an old linen shirt and the blue kilt around his hips. Even with her leg over him, the shirt came off in an instant, shredded fabric fluttering to the floor. The kilt followed, another tear rending the air so that seconds later he stood naked in his boots before her.

She glanced down, and that hint of amusement he'd come to expect flitted across her eyes.

Shit. He realized where she was going the second before she said it. "You call me Puss in Boots, and I swear I'll tan your backside."

Addie blinked, all sweetness and innocence. "Would I do that, my laird?"

"In an instant," Damon drawled.

He lifted her off the ladder to the closest flat surface, which was a large oak desk. A sheaf of blank paper and a stapler blocked his way, and he shoved them aside mindlessly. The stapler hit the floor first with the papers fluttering after, but his attention was on removing her clothing. She was as eager as him, jerking off her top as he expertly undid her bra strap and flung it behind them. Seconds later she was naked as well.

Oh God, she was naked, and she was gorgeous, and it was a good thing they'd already had some foreplay, because this boat was leaving, now. He caught hold of her hips, jerked her to the edge of the table, lined up his cock and buried himself deep.

"*Damon*." Her shout echoed off the high ceilings, and he froze.

She was still smiling.

Her mouth hung open, a haze of lust drifting into her gold-tinged eyes. "Laird Wolf. Have your way with me," she begged.

Damon lost it. He caught hold of her hips, thrust forward again and again, pressing a hand to the table as he pounded into her willing body. He still wore his black leather boots, but other than that they were both naked as the day they were born, solid grunts and cries of ecstasy escaping their lips.

Addie took him. Accepted him, hell, she urged him on, reaching forward and scratching her nails down his back as he leaned over her.

This was the man. It wasn't the wolf side of him. That beast remained hidden, and while Damon didn't understand it—his wolf enjoyed sex is much as any animal—he wasn't about to go looking for the creature. Right now he was focused on the woman under him, willing, and eager, and all too mesmerizing. He pulled out and stilled himself, his cock aimed at the entrance to her body. They were both breathing heavily, her chest shaking on every gasp.

She licked her lips. "Don't stop, make me sing."

He had every intention of doing that, but first...

Damon flipped her, resting her chest on the table as he leaned over and dusted a kiss on the back of her neck. "Is this okay?" he whispered, breaking character for a moment.

In answer, she stretched her hands above her on the table, placing herself under his complete control. "*Ooh*, are you going to punish me, my laird?" she teased.

All the blood drained from his head and went straight to his already impossibly hard cock as she egged him on in the most wicked way. He kissed his way down her spine until his lips met her lower back where the sweet swell of her ass began. "You've been disobedient, but I'll teach you to behave."

He rubbed a hand over her ass then brought it down with a sharp snap. Her creamy skin warmed against his palm, and the little gasp that escaped her lips was all about pleasure.

He couldn't last long, but he would make sure they had fun. "You've been disobedient, haven't you?" he repeated.

"Yes, Laird Wolf."

"I'm going to fuck your cunt hard so you know who it belongs to now."

"Yes, Laird Wolf." Breathless. Excited.

He struck again, his left hand this time, a sharp resounding snap hanging in the air followed by a moan from her lips.

He spanked her a couple more times, but it was all in play, and when she wiggled back, nudging the erection set firmly between her legs, he took the hint and slid inside.

They both sighed happily.

Addie glanced out of the corner of her eye, smiling sweetly. "Finish storming the castle."

He rocked forward, slowly at first before increasing speed. He pushed one of her legs onto the table, spreading her wide, his cock driving deeper, and a sound of satisfaction escaped.

It became part of the rhythm of sex. *Groan*, withdraw, thrust, *sigh*, withdraw, thrust, cry of pleasure.

She broke, shaking under him, and that was all he needed. Damon lost control and came, slipping free of her body and shooting his seed over her rounded ass cheeks. He pumped himself to get every last drop, eager spray flying up her back until ribbons of white marked her brown skin.

He fell forward, barely catching himself in time, hands

slapping on the hard tabletop as his breath raced, his brain gone foggy. She lay still, panting as hard as him, the fingers of her right hand tangled in his as they tried to recover.

"I have been thoroughly debauched," Addie finally declared. "Oh, woe is me."

Damon couldn't resist. He pressed his palm to her skin and slowly rubbed his seed in. "I'm marking you like the animal I am," he growled, loving the shiver that raced across her skin. "I've taken charge of all items of value here, and you, my lady, are what I claim as my reward."

He pulled her off the table and into his arms, lowering them into the nearest chair because his legs really weren't strong enough to hold them both up.

She glanced down, smirking as she realized he was still wearing nothing more than his boots. "You know, instead of Laird Wolf, maybe we *should* call you—"

Damon pressed his lips over hers to stop her from saying it, capturing her laugh with his mouth as he smiled. It had been a fine day, pillaging and all.

He wasn't minding this excursion to Scotland. Not one bit.

10

─────────

$\mathcal{A}$ ddie fought for air.

Wild, hopeless fear enveloped her, and she wiggled, trapped by strong, muscular limbs that seemed determined to pin her to the bed.

She knew it was a nightmare, and the emotions weren't hers. That the images rushing through her brain might be frightening and soul chilling, but they couldn't really hurt her. They weren't *real*.

That knowledge didn't make it any better, though, as she lay cradled in Damon's arms. Whatever strange barrier had been between them, the one that had allowed her to touch him without being swamped by emotion, the barrier was failing.

It wasn't a dissonance of raw emotion swamping her like she'd received from Niall the other week. More a slow trickle, memories building one on top of the other, jangled images and strong feelings of guilt and sadness. Agonizing, crushing loss.

All of it came from Damon, and she rolled to face him, terrified the situation might get worse. Even more terrified she might not be able to help him. She twisted away as a memory struck as sharp as a physical blow.

The images continued to escalate in intensity, including flashes of men with ski masks over their faces, and a rising bloodlust. His emotion, not hers.

Damon's arm lay heavily over her body, their legs tangled together, and she fought down a whimper as she dragged herself free. After that day in the garden, they'd taken to sleeping together in their human forms. It had felt so good to have constant touch, and not have to worry about the consequences, but it seemed they'd been wrong.

She was desperate not to wake him, desperate not to have to explain why she was nearly sick to her stomach. He'd feel it was his fault for frightening her—she knew that's what he'd think, and it was the last thing she wanted.

Addie escaped from the bed, swamped by her own full-blown combination of relief and guilt.

Damon twitched in his sleep, his face folded in a grimace as if he was suffering.

That was the kicker. She knew *exactly* what he was feeling, the cause and the hurt. He was reliving that night he'd told her about—the night he'd lost Caitlin, and if she were brave she'd hold him and take away his pain, but she was so afraid.

Torn by indecision, Addie hesitated. Yet one heartbreaking cry later, she couldn't take it any longer. No matter what the cost, she had to help him.

Addie crawled back on the bed, took a deep breath, and laid her hand on his chest.

Darkness and pain swept over her. *His pain. His loss.*

She gritted her teeth. She could take it away. A little effort, and the memories would fade, and his distress would diminish, but to do so without his permission was hugely invasive.

But she couldn't bear to leave him suffering, so she did the only other thing possible.

She took it all herself.

No longer did pain dance on the surface of her mind like the heat of a distant fire against her skin. Instead, a set of red-hot daggers struck deep. Temporary relief for him meant temporary agony for her. She went from sharing his hurt to carrying it alone, and the weight threatened to make her pass out...

...and his wolf arrived. The secretive beast she'd only caught the faintest glimpses of over the past week.

Mine.

Mine.

The simultaneous announcement came from the wolf inside her *and* from Damon's wolf. While she struggled to understand, the animal within Damon offered his power and his strength and his support. And all she could do was the mental equivalent of a jaw drop.

Damon was her *mate?*

The shock of it was huge, but there was no time to wonder because as much as the beast wanted to help, this moment was all on her and there was no turning back.

She swept through Damon's mind, drawing away all the suffering she found. Addie forced herself to remain under the cutting pain, taking the punishment for him.

The entire time his wolf howled and roared in her ears, ordering her to stop. Demanding she wake Damon's human side so they could deal with this together.

Fat chance. He might be an Alpha, but she'd been dealing with emotional chaos for a long time, and while the new knowledge Damon was her mate was awesome, and amazing, and *incredible*, she was powerful enough to fight his wolf's command and finish what she'd begun.

It should have ruined her. Should have taken all her energy and left her head aching and her soul torn, but somehow, even as she drew off the hurt from Damon, the other parts of them helped carry the burden. Their wolf sides soothing the pain as well.

She'd never experienced anything like it—and joy rippled through her.

Damon and their wolves made her stronger.

Then the sweet, soft caress of her wolf shifted focus to nudge against Damon's other side. Calming his beast, distracting him until the man before her stopped shaking. Until the animal side took a deep breath and gave in as well to the suggestion to sleep.

Not until Damon's face relaxed and she was positive both he and his wolf rested peacefully did Addie draw back her hand to stare in amazement. For whatever reason, the barrier between them was gone, and they were *mates*.

Her heart still pounded, and she should have felt exhausted from what she'd just done, but *glory hallelujah*, she and Damon were mates and she could have run a marathon, she had so much energy.

But as much as she wanted to bounce on the bed and shout out loud to make sure he knew as well, she couldn't bear to wake him. Not when he'd finally relaxed, the faintest of smiles curling his lips. Her mate needed to sleep.

Her mate. The wonder of it boggled her.

She slipped on clothes, escaping from the room before she was tempted to change her mind. The morning would be soon enough to discuss their incredible, while whacky, change of situation. In the meantime, she was awake; she might as well do something productive.

Addie all but danced down the stairs and the hall, glancing around instinctively as she went to be sure no one else was awake. She headed back to the library, her middle-of-the-night still-jumbled thoughts drifting as she passed through long, empty halls.

She propped a pile of books in the doorway to make sure there were no further accidental locked-in incidents.

But instead of getting straight to work, she wandered. Wonder and amazement keeping her from her tasks.

There was no use trying to figure out why they hadn't recognized each other as mates right away. She had to wait until morning for that answer.

Instead, she got caught up in anticipation. Not about here and now, but the future. That they were mates—it explained so much. The draw she'd felt to him, the craving to touch. And after getting to be with Damon, to play with him and enjoy his company, she was so grateful she didn't have to give him up.

She had fallen for him hard, and in the big picture of wolves and mates and all the rest, that was like the icing on an enormous cake she was about to gorge herself on for the rest of their lives.

He was a good man. She liked his sense of humour and the way he cared for her. The way he looked at her whenever they were together, the intent focus in those blue eyes that made her feel as if she was the most important thing in his world.

Together they could find a way to deal with her weirdo wolfie ways, she was sure of it.

Her gaze drifted as she pondered, settling on a row of golden leather journals lined up at the top of the first-storey bookcase.

Something itched at the base of her spine, like a

memory wanting to burst free. A second later it rushed her —those strange journals she'd been seeing everywhere. She'd assumed the scattered books were part of a set, and now that she saw the others, she was certain of it. The tone of the spine, the distinctive leather cover—

But there wasn't enough room on the shelf to fit the number of books dispersed all over the manor.

Damn fool.

It hadn't been a half dozen misplaced leather journals she'd seen—it was the *same* journal that had shown up all over the place, although how on earth the book had skipped from place to place, and why, she had no idea.

Maybe the rest of the set would offer a clue. Addie hurried toward the bookshelf, smiling in remembrance of her and Damon's earlier adventures on the ladder as she slid it into position and climbed. The row of golden-skinned tomes sat regally, all there except for one, the narrow gap where it should have been mocking her.

She was reaching for one of the remaining books to examine it when something crashed against the outer wall of the manor.

She slipped down the ladder, heart pounding and made her way to the window, surprised to find it propped open. She poked her head out in time to see a shadowy figure disappear around the nearby angled roof section.

Holy moly, she'd been right about the weird goings-on around the place. Addie crawled on the windowsill and out onto the wide, fairly flat rooftop behind it. She wasn't getting in over her head—she promised herself to stay far back and out of danger. But someone had been in the room, and after all of those times of feeling as if she was being watched, she wanted to know who it was.

Besides, she was a freaking wolf shifter. Her wolf's

hackles went up, and her teeth itched to appear. If someone wanted to mess with her, they would have one pissed-off lupine on their hands.

Out on the roof, she inched forward until she could poke her head over the edge to peek at the balcony below her. A tall, robed figure clung to the railing, staring down toward the courtyard. The wind rushed past and his hood fell away to reveal blond hair. She forced her lips together, holding in her anger, wondering what Niall was up to.

The wind shifted, and a new scent reached her. Familiar, and completely out of place. Addie turned away from Niall and went tracking.

DAMON WOKE, totally confused by the sense of urgency clawing at him. The bed was soft and comfortable, and he stretched slowly, not wanting to disturb Addie.

Only she was gone, and the empty space beside him was cold to his touch. A quick examination of the entire room proved she was nowhere in sight.

Inside, his wolf was no longer hiding in the dungeon or wherever it had banished itself for the past week. The beast was right there rattling the chains, wanting out. Wanting to protect, needing to seek out and find their—

Mate.

Holy fucking *shit.*

Damon jerked to a stop outside of the tower room, shocked at what his wolf was all but howling at him, wondering how in the hell he hadn't known until this moment.

Wondering how in the hell it could be true.

He raced down the stairs, jumping the last section and

landing in a crouch as he teetered on the line between human and animal. Something was wrong, Addie was in trouble.

He had no idea how he knew, but he knew, and the idea he had failed her sent nausea rolling through him like a flash fire before it was burned up by ferocious anger.

He should have been protecting her. He *could* have protected her if his damn wolf hadn't been hiding. Hadn't been keeping fucking *secrets*.

Damon hit the main level, following her scent toward the next staircase when he caught a glimpse of a furry body ahead of him.

He lunged after the beast, catching up with the oversized cat and grabbing its tail. The animal screamed and shifted, transforming into a very agitated Alastair.

Holy shit, *that's* all a Highland Tiger was? A glorified pussycat?

"Where's Addie?" Damon demanded, claws emerging as he wrapped a hand around Alastair's throat.

His enemy's eyes bulged. "I haven't seen her, I swear," he squealed, hands clutching Damon's fingers, scrambling to loosen his grip.

"What are you doing skulking about in the middle of the night?"

"I was following my brother. He's up...to no good. He's always up to no good. Can't..." Alastair slapped feebly at Damon's iron-hard grip, "...breathe."

Damon forced himself to let go, stepping in close and peering down from his full height as the other man shrank before him. "If either of you have done anything to hurt her, I will rip you apart." His voice going slower and deeper until the words became a bloody promise.

Alastair shook his head, retreating as rapidly as possible.

"She went upstairs earlier, but I didn't go near her, I swear. Please don't hurt me."

Damon gave in to his beast, shifting so his senses were as keen as possible. He put his nose down and followed her scent toward the library where he found the door open and her iPad abandoned on the table.

The trail led to the window, and he shifted back to human so he could scramble onto the rooftop. "Sweetheart, what the hell are you doing?" he whispered, fear a bitter taste on his tongue.

He circled the rooftop and found Niall's scent, and the sound that came from his throat was pure wolf. An animal cry as the beast remembered too much pain, too much loss.

Not again, he reassured his wolf. They were not going to lose her.

The beast wanted blood, but revenge wasn't the most important thing. Damon slapped his wolf into submission and instead of following Niall's trail, he reversed direction. Searching until he found the subtle scent where Addie had turned aside and gone down a different rooftop and over a small parapet to a balcony. He moved rapidly, breaking into a room where another one of the hidden passages he'd found began.

Addie hadn't been alone. As he hurried down the narrow stairs to the ground level, rushing into the cool morning air, he memorized the other scent. When this was over and he had her safely back, he would track down his enemy and give them the death they so clearly deserved for coming near his mate.

The wolf that was Damon sped after her as dawn brightened the eastern sky. His paws smacked into the earth in a rapid rhythm, and the entire time the most impossible words repeated over and over.

Mate. Mate. Mine.

He wasn't about to argue with the beast. Once he knew which direction they were headed, he let the animal take control, rushing them forward, seeking their goal. Damon darted through the gate at the far end of the estate, the scent increasing as he drew closer to the small group of homesteaders' cottages. He moved into the shadows, ducking behind rose bushes until he reached the door of the cottage he'd been in before.

Even as he shifted to human, he stifled the growl in his throat. His target was somewhere on the other side. He heard Glenn's voice, waiting only long enough to be sure Addie was there as well before he kicked open the door, springing forward into the room like an avenging demon from hell.

They whirled to face him. Glenn shot to his feet and threw a protective arm in front of his grandmam. Damon marched forward, stalking them, murder on his mind.

Then Addie was there, standing between him and the others as her whisky-coloured eyes tempted him to focus on her alone.

"Damon. Stop." She laid a hand on his chest, and he caught her in his grip, circling her wrist carefully as he stared down at her, possessiveness flowing through his veins.

She blinked rapidly but held her ground as he forced the words past vocal cords that seemed none too human. "Are you hurt?"

"No." Her instant response reassured him, as did the tender touch of her fingers as she stroked his cheek. But her body shook, and for one horrifying second he thought she was afraid of him.

Then she jumped, wrapping her arms around his neck

as she clung to him and offered a kiss. Lips that were soft, and warm, and tempting. As her taste rolled through him, the flash of inspiration he'd gotten before became absolute and complete fact.

She was his damn *mate*.

She pulled away too soon, tilting her head as she smiled. "I was listening to a story."

What the hell? "At five in the morning?"

She nodded, slipping down his body but keeping her fingers locked in his as she tugged him toward the empty chair. Only in a group of shifters would the fact he was stark-naked not be an issue. She waved a hand reassuringly at Glenn, and he reluctantly returned to his seat.

"We're all okay. And Damon needs to hear this as well," Addie insisted, squeezing his fingers.

Glenn frowned. "Can we trust him?"

Damon took the chair and, unwilling to let her go, tugged her onto his lap and enveloped her in his arms, protecting her like a shield.

Yet as violent as he was prepared to be on her behalf, he could've been knocked over by a gnat as she spoke firmly in answer to Glenn. "Damon is my mate. I promise he'll do what's right."

Mate.

She'd said *mate*. He hadn't imagined it, and she knew as well, and *holy shit*.

Mine. Damon's wolf growled in satisfaction.

"Of course he'll do the right thing." Grandmam Susanna this time, the old woman nodding her head toward them as an eager smile broke out. She shook her finger at her grandson before pointing back and forth between Addie and Damon. "See what you're missing by not looking for true love?"

Glenn rolled his eyes before facing his grandmam. "Let's not talk about that."

She shook her head. "But that's what we *are* talking about, my darlin' grandson. It's love that makes us do foolish things at times. But it's love that makes things right in the end. I know that in here," and she laid a withered hand over her chest, smiling deeply.

The lines of her face spoke of years of history, but her attention was centered on the here and now. Whatever else was going on, the old woman was rational for the moment.

Damon stroked a hand down Addie's arm. What he wanted to do was figure out the mystery of how he had not *known*, but following Addie's gentle guidance, he did the only thing he could—he listened.

Although, they'd better make it fast. He had a shit-ton of questions to ask, and he wanted answers—*now*.

11

———

$\mathcal{A}$ ddie sat in Damon's lap, enveloped in a welcome whirlwind of sensory input.

She'd followed the trail all the way to the village, the scent growing stronger until she was sure of her mysterious person's identity.

But what Grandmam Susanna had been doing on the rooftops of the Sterling-Wylde manor, she hadn't a clue.

The cook vanished into her cottage before Addie caught up, and as she stood there, wondering what to do next, she'd been surprised by Glenn popping out the door. All it had taken was a single touch on his arm to confirm the only things on his mind were shock at seeing her and concern for his grandmam.

When she'd entered the small cottage and found the old woman going about her morning routine, she'd joined in, carefully slipping her fingers over Grandmam's as she passed a cup of tea.

A week ago, being touched by Niall had sent a roll of nausea through her, his overwhelming, self-centered lust a huge part of his personality. In contrast, what she received from Susanna was a gift of the purest kind.

The elderly fox-shifter was a woman full of love. Love for her grandson, love for her job. And over it all, a rich sense of selfless love, so sacrificial she was willing to give up her secrets to provide for others.

That small bit of Omega knowledge kept Addie in the cottage listening to the old woman's rambling stories to discover the real reason she'd been in the manor.

Damon was not supposed to appear like a Hound of Baskerville come to life. Correction—a very naked, very *fine* human beast with vengeance and fury in his eyes.

And now his muscular hands were wrapped around her so tightly she was sure he would never let go. The barrier between them had vanished, and the strongest emotion in him was absolute astonishment.

There were others. The attraction between them was powerful, with a fair share of lust that made her squirm in place before she carefully pushed it aside to enjoy later. His enormous attraction didn't make her uncomfortable because it was a combination of desire and enjoyment. It included a thrill of delight as he considered ways to be together in pleasure *and* play.

And for the first time she understood the strange sensation she'd always felt from him—his wolf in hiding. Hiding to keep the truth from coming out, although she still had no idea why.

They were *mates*, and she wanted to dance with joy because it was perfect.

Once they left the cottage they would deal with the ravaging fear that had taken him in the night, but right now it was time to solve another mystery. She pressed her hand to Damon's cheek, and her wolf bumped against his. Calming him, and promising she was his.

Some of the tension drained from his shoulders, and he took a deep breath, nuzzling his nose against her ear. Then he looked her in the eye, and she knew this would never be over, this thing between them. Not ever.

He linked his fingers in hers, turning to face the room. "Grandmam Susanna. You speak about love as if you know it well."

Glenn stiffened, but Grandmam nodded, pouring a cup of tea for Damon and bringing it to him, her sunshiny smile beaming on them all. "I did know love, and he was magnificent."

"A mate?"

"No. We fox don't take mates, not like you wolves. In some ways I'm jealous, because I understand it's like nothing I've ever experienced." She patted Damon on the shoulder as if he were a child. "But then, I've truly and deeply loved more than one man, and that's something you wolves simply can't understand, so we'll call it even."

"Grandmam." Glenn sounded scandalized.

"Oh, hush, boy. I know I'm old and dried up now, but I wasn't always." She met Addie's eye and offered a wink. "Children think they're the first ones to ever have discovered sex. I don't know how they think they got here if that's the case."

Glenn dropped his face into his hands, his shoulders shaking as he laughed.

Damon's voice rumbled up from deep in his chest as he gently questioned the old woman who'd returned to her seat. "And did you have a lover at the manor?"

She nodded, pulling a locket from beneath her lace

shawl and holding it in the palm of her hand. She stroked it with her fingertips. "My Lachlan gave this to me. He wanted to marry me, you know, but I didn't want all the troubles that would cause, him and I being so different. It was best for both of us to stay where we were. But our brief time together was delightful. My heart and home are full of memories."

"What if you have to leave the manor?" Damon asked cautiously.

Glenn cleared his throat. "I'm hoping whoever takes ownership might find it in their heart to keep us on for a little longer." He slammed his lips together but looked beseechingly at Addie, as if begging her to read his mind.

"Oh dear, we have guests." Grandmam brushed her hands together then straightened her skirt as she rose to her feet and came forward, offering her hands to Addie and Damon. "So good to meet you. I'm Susanna, and this is my grandson, Glenn. Would you like to come in and have a cup of tea?"

Without a word Damon gently placed Addie on the ground, standing and accepting Grandmam's hand. "It's wonderful to meet you," he said. "I'm Damon, and this is my mate, Addie. We'll be working at the manor for the next while."

She clasped her hands together in delight. "Oh, the *manor*. I have a job there, you know. I might see you." She tucked a stray grey hair behind her ear and winked at Damon with a touch of sauciness. "I hope I see you around, young man. I do like pretty boys."

Then she marched away, disappearing into a back room, singing all the while.

Glenn stood, clutching his cup and looking embarrassed, and then frightened as if he realized there was no shield between him and Damon. "I'm so sorry about that."

Addie waved away the apology. "Sometimes she remembers more than others, right?"

"And sometimes her memory vanishes when I least expect. Or she'll behave in unpredictable ways." His hands twisted before him as if he were begging. "Please, you're not upset with her, are you?"

Damon snapped up a finger, pointing to the chair behind Glenn and he rushed to obey, sitting instantly. Addie thought she'd take the third chair but Damon was having nothing of it, tugging her into his lap as they settled back in place.

"I think you'd better tell us the whole story."

Glenn swallowed hard, glancing between the two of them before nodding, his chin rising as if he had sucked in all the bravery possible. "After Lord Sterling-Wylde died, and we found out what the sons' plans were for the estate, I overheard Grandmam while she was visiting his grave. She told him she had to share their secret."

His eyes flashed as Addie jerked upright in surprise.

"My father was a by-blow of that love affair she mentioned, but until that moment, I'd never known. And our family never had any issue working for Lord Sterling-Wylde. Lachlan was a good man, very different from his sons.

"My grandmother showed me the locket and a box of papers he'd given her once upon a time. I thought they were all love letters, but the one on the top turned out to be a will he'd given her shortly before he died."

Under her, Damon stiffened. "And does this will name a different inheritor?"

Glenn nodded slowly. "I was afraid to give it to Niall or Alastair for fear they'd destroy it."

"But why didn't you give it straight to the authorities?" Addie asked.

Damon stroked his fingers down her arm again, the sense of wonder and rightness of the motion sinking in like intoxicating wine. "Because the love affair was secret," he murmured. "It would raise more questions than you had answers, and you wanted to protect your grandmam."

The other man hesitated. "It doesn't help that Grandmam doesn't always know what day it is, or what year. It's one thing for a new, mysterious will to appear, giving the entire inheritance to the workers who cared for Lord Sterling-Wylde during his last twenty years. That will create gossip all on its own, and that's fine. But for it to show up in the hands of a man who looks suspiciously like a relative, especially next to the pictures in the grand hallway... There's no way her secret could possibly remain hidden."

Damon chuckled. "I wish I would've met Lord Sterling-Wylde. He sounds like a very sneaky man. That's brilliant, you know. Give the estate to a group of people, and not the one person he doesn't want to draw attention to."

"But is it legal?" Addie asked.

Damon hesitated. "I wouldn't know even if I looked at the will, but I can promise to get it to the right people to find out."

Glenn reached under his shirt and pulled out a linen envelope. "After Addie arrived and handed over the wills she discovered, I thought that was my solution. I tried hiding it where you would find it, but I had to keep moving it out of fear that Niall or Alastair would discover it first."

Of course. "You put it in the yellow leather journal I

found scattered all over the house. I can't believe I didn't figure it out sooner."

Damon caught her by the chin. He pressed a brief kiss to her lips, a wave of comfort and a hint of laughter wrapping around her like a warm blanket. "Don't blame yourself. It was a good attempt by Glenn, and you would've found it eventually."

The other man smiled ruefully. "Except Grandmam got tired of my 'sloppy attempts' so she decided to go herself."

"Over the rooftops?" Addie asked in astonishment.

He made another face. "Told me she knew all the secret ways in and out of the manor. I don't want to think about why. But she planned to put it right where you would be sure to find it."

"Let me guess. She spotted Niall and changed her mind?"

Glenn nodded.

The entire story was twisted and crazy, and made complete sense.

Damon offered a hand. "Why don't you give me the will? We should get it where it belongs as soon as possible."

The precious papers were passed over, and Addie took them with a sigh of satisfaction, rising to her feet and waiting for Damon.

Glenn picked up a folded tartan from a nearby shelf and tossed it to him. "You're welcome to this. Along with our thanks."

"Nothing is guaranteed, but we'll do our best," Damon promised, and then they were gone, rushed from the cottage so quickly Addie barely had time to wave goodbye.

~

Wearing another borrowed kilt around his hips, Damon kept a firm grip on Addie's fingers as he all but raced down a secret passage he'd found that led from the nearby watchtower ruins to the library. There they paused. He had one detail to deal with before they could get to the most important discussion of his life.

"Phone number for the executor."

She found it for him on her iPad, waiting quietly as he used the manor's landline to leave a message on the law-office answering machine. Then she came willingly as he led her back into the darkness of the tunnels, taking the shortest route he knew to the base of her tower.

"I had no idea this was here," she whispered into the still of the morning.

"I found it the other day. There must be dozens of others I don't know about yet. I wonder how many we'll find in the end?"

"We could ask Grandmam Susanna." Addie sounded impressed with the secret liaison. "That was my favourite part of the story."

"Seems we're not the only ones who've heated up parts of the manor in scandalous ways." Keeping it together until they had privacy took most of his concentration, and talking about tunnels was better than nothing. "I don't want to chance running into the boys. Why didn't you warn me they're nothing more than a common house cat?"

Addie blinked in surprise. "That's what Highland Tigers are. I thought you knew."

Damon shook his head. "I want to kick their furry butts for all those times I didn't realize they were the ones hanging around being annoying." They were halfway up the stairs, and she kept squeezing her fingers around his as if trying to confirm he was really there.

He led her through the bedroom, dropping the will on the dresser before heading onto the east balcony toward the oversized chairs he'd put there a few days ago.

When she made a move toward the second chair he spun her, holding her tightly. "Not so fast. We have some talking to do."

Addie nodded. "I'm not sure where to begin."

"I do." He cupped her face in his hands and drew her in for a blistering kiss, taking her mouth as if he owned it, which, *hello*, he totally did. Just like she owned every bit of him, from then till forever.

It was the wolf inside that gave him the strength to pull away, the beast nudging him apologetically while insisting the talking thing might be a good idea before the claiming began.

Damon sighed. "I don't know why all of a sudden *he* decides he has to be the reasonable one."

She curled her fingers against his chest. "Your wolf?"

That side of him rushed upward, trying to reach Addie. Damon got ready to fight the beast back, but before he could say a thing she responded. She whispered soothingly, petting his chest as she led him to the nearest chair and somehow ended with her curled up in his lap.

His wolf settled into a bundle of contentment, and Damon eyed her with trepidation. "That was...weird."

Addie offered an apologetic smile. "Get used to weird. Since we're mates, and all, it seems we'll have plenty of time to learn each other's little foibles."

"How can that be?" It still made no sense, although... "I mean, I'm so glad, and I'm not giving you up, but how the *hell* did I miss something as big as this between us?"

She stroked his cheek, resting her head against his

shoulder. "I'm not sure, not completely, but I have a couple of ideas."

As long as she didn't stop touching him, he could talk this out. "It's karma rewarding us?"

"Maybe it has to do with what you told me about with Caitlin."

It was a good thing she was still petting him, because his wolf was too calm to fly off the handle like he normally would have at the mention of that night. Instead, Damon held her, and thought it through.

"I can feel what you're feeling," she whispered.

He froze. "Am I hurting you?"

She laughed, sitting up and meeting his gaze. "I knew that would be the first thing you'd ask. No, I'm not being overwhelmed. It's as if your wolf side and mine, now that they know we have each other, they're running just enough interference I can touch you without repercussions. But I can sense far more from you than before."

Damon hesitated. "You feel my wolf, as well?"

Addie nodded, a smile breaking free. "I told you I looked forward to meeting him."

Son of a gun. "You couldn't sense my wolf up to now."

She shook her head, golden sparkles in her eyes dancing back at him.

"That's it. My wolf was hiding," Damon muttered. "Damn beast refused to let me know why, and all this time it seemed he was hiding from *you.*"

"And because he was hiding, we didn't know we were mates." The little crease between her eyes deepened. "Which explains the *how*, but I don't understand *why*. Why on earth would he do that?"

Damon swore lightly, realization sinking in. "He was protecting you, but not because of anything you've done, but because of me. Because of him. Oh *damn*, it all makes sense."

He was tempted to pull away to save her the rush of sorrow that was about to arrive as he revisited the past and the night he'd lost Caitlin. Another wave of guilt struck, one he would never be free of.

He'd never wanted to forget because his mistake had cost Caitlin everything, but now it seemed it had almost cost him Addie, and that was unacceptable.

"That night when she died, I got reckless, and let the wolf take control. That was why I didn't step back when I should have. And since then we've never gotten along, him and I. Always fighting for dominance, and because we fight, I'm not a complete wolf. If I can't control myself, how can I be there for others who need me? Like you, or a pack, or..." He trailed off, lost in her whisky-coloured gaze.

"Oh, Damon." She whispered his name, fingers stroking his cheek as she tipped her lips toward him and pressed her mouth to his briefly. A sweet benediction that offered forgiveness and a future, all at the same time. "I'm so sorry you lost her, but I'll never be sorry I get to have you as mine."

Emotion choked his throat. "My God, what if I did something that hurt you?"

She squeezed his arms as the flecks of gold in her eyes grew brighter. "You can't hurt me except if you give me less than all of yourself. You're an amazing wolf, Damon, and I look forward to getting to know you better during the years we have ahead of us. I will not let you hide your wolf away ever again. I want all of you. I deserve all of you."

So perfect for him, this complicated woman full of fury and laughter and...

Emotion.

That's what was missing.

He caught her chin in his hand and stared at her intently. His wolf rushed in, wanting to help this time. Willing to do anything to make sure Addie was safe, but more than that, that she was happy.

Since she was theirs.

Mate his wolf insisted.

Yes, our *mate. And we will protect her, and care for her,* Damon answered back, the battle between them easing as they united behind one goal.

That's when his wolf gave him the rundown on what happened only hours earlier. Damon's heart stuttered at hearing she'd suffered while helping him—and why the fuck hadn't she told him?

She was keeping secrets, and it was time for *all* the secrets to be out in the open.

"Let's make this clear, right here and now, Addie MacShay. I'm your mate, and I want all of you, as well."

Her face lit up like sunshine.

He leaned in and brushed his lips over hers. "Which means no more nighttime martyr-tricks."

"Shit." She blinked guiltily. "How did you know? Did you remember...?" Her eyes narrowed, her fingers tightening on his shoulder where her hand rested. A cool sensation brushed his mind, like the sweep of butterfly wings. "Your wolf. *Bastard.* He snitched. He's as much trouble as you are!"

"You were going to tell me, weren't you?" Damon demanded.

"Yes, but..."

"Then what's the problem?"

She opened her mouth and then closed it quickly. "No problem."

He kissed her again, deepening his touch as he satisfied just a hint of his craving.

A sigh of pleasure escaped her, fading as he pulled back and stared into her eyes. "Tell me. Tell me what you're still not saying."

She nodded slowly. "I eased your pain last night. I can do more than that."

"Not if it's going to hurt you."

"It won't. I mean, it shouldn't."

He glared at her.

She glared back, then pulled a funny face and set him laughing in spite of everything that was going on.

Amazing woman. Amazing, and just as stubborn as he was—their life was never going to be boring. "I want *all* of you, Addie. Every single bit, and whatever gifts make you unique—I accept them. Don't hold back on me."

It was her turn to stare wordlessly for a moment. "Are you sure?"

"Definitely—"

It was like a gate opened on a dam, and he felt her touch not just where her hand rested, but inside, as if the edges of their souls were meshing together while Addie swept in.

He recognized her soft, caring caress as it soothed the ragged edges of his memories. She petted him, comforted him, then slapped him around a little for the guilt he still carried. But she didn't try to tug it away, and he was glad because he needed to remember. He never wanted Caitlin to completely be gone, yet Addie left him the good memories while softening the pain.

And then he sat, head spinning as she breathed out a happy sigh.

"Holy shit, that was amazing," he said, wonder in his voice.

"When I mess with someone's emotions, I *really* mess with them, right?" She didn't give him time to respond, instead pressing her lips to his and leaning their bodies together. "I want to..." she whispered against his lips, "...know what it's like to be with my mate."

Damon shook as the intensity of her statement sank in, as her sheer love and acceptance met him head-on.

He rose, carrying her into the bedroom.

12

Talk about life-changing experiences.

Somehow between the last time she'd gone to bed and being lowered carefully onto it now, she'd tracked down a missing will and heirs, soothed a man who'd suffered for years...

And found her mate.

Damon covered her with his body. It was the heaven she'd been hoping for.

But she didn't want to hurry. Touching him, sharing completely intimate skin-on-skin experiences would be amazing, but to rush forward without considering all the new nuances between them seemed criminal.

She pressed her hands to his bare chest, caressing strong muscles as she stared into his eyes. "I need to touch you everywhere."

"That's my line," he rumbled, dipping his head to brush their mouths together. His lips traveled across her cheek until he was nibbling her earlobe. She leaned into him, her entire body one huge bundle of sensitive desire.

His emotions filtered through her, distinct and uniquely

his. As individual as his handwriting, or the familiar glide of his fingers down her torso so he could play with her breast—that was Damon, that was how *he* caressed her.

And now his thoughts and emotions did the same thing—they wrote a message inside, just for her to read. Passion and lust, but the desire wasn't invasive because it was passion and adoration all at once. As if he couldn't believe she was his for the touching. He would never tire of her. It would take their entire lives for this need to begin to be met.

"I'll always be there for you," Damon promised, sliding back so his hips settled between her thighs.

His eyes weren't sky-blue anymore. Now his human side mixed with the silver of his wolf, both of them rising up and promising protection. Promising Damon would be everything she needed him to be.

She captured his face with her hands so she could kiss him until she was lightheaded, oxygen-deprived but sustained by a steady stream of life-giving emotion pouring off of him into her very soul.

Damon rolled to the side, pulling off his kilt in one motion, his strong biceps flexing as he moved to grab the bottom of her shirt and jerk it over her head. The fabric was tossed aside as he went for her pants, stripping her bare in a matter of seconds as he stared in wide-eyed adoration.

"I can't believe you're mine."

"Always," she promised in return. "To help you, to support you and love you."

He pulled her into his arms. "I like the sound of that. It's what I've always wanted."

The emotion pouring from him matched his words, but there was more. Things that words alone couldn't say that were concealed deep inside. Maybe Damon wasn't aware what else he'd been hiding for too long, and she wasn't about to blurt them out. But he had to know one thing.

"You're not *just* mine." She nestled closer, settling in his lap, their torsos touching, his arms wrapped around her as she ran her fingers through his hair. "I want you, and I need you, but I'm not so selfish as to keep you all to myself when there's more that *you* need."

A shudder took him for an instant, but inside his wolf howled in agreement, the beast damn near grinning at the thought of getting to care for an actual pack. That was what it craved, what *they* needed to be complete. Until that happened, Damon would never truly be happy either.

He tucked his fingers under her chin and tipped her head back. "Enough of you being curled up inside my head. We'll talk about all sorts of things in the days to come, but right now I want you."

She had no objections. She had even less when he lifted her enough he could nuzzle her breasts. Teasing and taunting until he rolled her under him and slid down her body to make her system sing.

He seemed determined to make her see stars, and she really couldn't fight his single-minded focus on turning her into a pile of quivering jelly. Breathing grew tough when her entire body shook for the third time in rapid succession.

"My turn," she said, attempting to twist free to touch him as well.

"Nothing doing." Damon scooped her up and paced to the nearest wall. "Well, okay, you can do one thing."

She wrapped her arms and legs around him instinctively, the thick heat of his cock settling against just the right spot. "I have no idea what."

"I'll tell you when the moment is right." Damon pushed her backward and down, spearing her on his hard length.

Glorious sensation rippled through her as his thickness spread her wide, and she dug in her fingernails.

His hands protected her from the cold stone wall, while the hot, hard cock he thrust into her over and over was enough to make her drop her head back and moan in ecstasy.

"So good. Yes, my mate."

"*Mine*," Damon agreed, rocking again with a grunt of satisfaction.

He found a way to reach between them, teasing her clit with his fingertips as he drove into her. Pleasure twirled faster until she was on the very edge. One more thing would tip her over—

His teeth at her neck, biting down. Marking her and claiming her as his and, oh my *God*. Her climax hit, and the tower room was in danger of exploding, torn from the foundation and shot into the heavens.

Satisfaction didn't pulse through her veins; it ricocheted like ten million ping-pong balls all launched at once into a confined space.

Addie fought her way out from her pleasure-induced state of euphoria and put her mouth to his shoulder, licking daintily as she struggled to catch her breath for long enough to complete the ritual.

Damon drove his cock deeper, beads of sweat forming on his forehead as he leaned one elbow on the wall and shortened his stroke. Keeping close enough for her to reach.

"God, Addie, *now*," he begged.

She snapped her jaws shut. His taste raced over her tongue, and the connection they'd forged through her Omega talent widened further as the mate bond snapped into place.

Damon shouted, hips thrust forward one last time before stilling, buried deep inside her. His body inside hers.

Their minds inside each others.

"Oh man, that was intense." Damon's voice. Inside her head.

Addie kissed his cheek, his shoulder, everything she could reach. "That was amazing."

Powerful arms cradled her as if she were the most precious thing in his world. Powerful emotion wrapped around them—love and friendship and belonging, all tangled together.

He stood there, nuzzling her neck until she squirmed against him, the heat between them flaring again. Damon stepped away from where he'd been leaning, his fiery gaze darting over her as he took her to the shower and proceeded to make love to her all over again. "It's going to take some getting used to, this whole mate thing," he warned.

Addie leaned on the shower wall and admired the tall, muscular wolf in front of her who was hers, now and forever. *"That's why we're mates. We have all the time in the world."*

It took enormous effort to get up a few hours later, not just because her bed was warm and comfortable, but because it was full of eager male wolf with every intention of proving his claim again and again until she laughingly escaped his grasp.

"Damon, stop. I have to get to work. And the executor should be here in a few hours."

He waggled his brows. "I like having a mate," he

exhaled on a sigh, leaning back on the pillows and folding his hands behind his head.

"You look like a cat that's gotten into the cream."

His face twitched. "Oh, hell, *no*. Stop right now with the cat jokes."

"Should we get matching collars?" Addie teased as she pulled on her clothes, barely escaping as he bounded after her with a snarling laugh.

They hadn't solved everything, but for two wolves the biggest issue had already been settled. They would be together from now on, period. That was unquestionable, and the rest of it they would work out in the coming weeks.

"I'll deal with the will first thing," Damon told her, tucking it away carefully before pulling her back into his arms for a body-shaking kiss.

They were both grinning like fools when she finally wiggled free. "I'll get back to work. Join me when you can."

She happily headed to the library, content to finish her task while she trusted Damon to fulfill his promise.

Addie was so into her work it was only by chance she noticed a long, black sedan pull into the yard. When she recognized the executor, she couldn't resist. She grabbed her things and raced downstairs, slipping outside before the man reached the front doors.

She tucked herself behind one of the massive entrance pillars. A warm hand slipped into hers, briefly squeezed her fingers, then Damon stepped forward, joining Niall and Alastair on the front step as the business-suited man approached.

Niall sniffed. "Really, don't you have somewhere else you need to be? Bones to dig up, or balls to chase?"

Damon chuckled, a touch of evil in the tone. "Oh, I've been digging up bones, all right. Wait and see."

Alastair spotted her, his eyes widening as he took a cautionary step away from Damon.

The executor arrived at the base of the stairs, glancing up expectantly. "I hear you have news for me."

Niall sneered. "Please. After all this time, you should have news for us. You haven't come to a decision?"

The man offered Niall a disdainful glance. "We're working through the other wills, but I understood there was a new one. A newer one than any we're examining, and obviously less fabricated than at least two of the others we have on file."

Alastair choked. "Fabricated—that's preposterous."

"Is it?" the man asked, a single brow rising. "It's a criminal offense to forge legal documents, you know. Perhaps we'll just ignore that small matter if this new will is less fake than the ones you and your brother handed in to the office."

"I think you'll find this authentic." Damon stepped forward, the blue-and-green tartan around his hips flaring slightly as he handed the executor the precious papers Glenn had shared.

Alastair and Niall screeched like cats being tossed in a lake.

"What are you doing?" Niall made the mistake of grabbing for the papers.

Damon snapped at him. "Addie found it in the library. I assumed you'd want it given to the proper authorities."

Alastair glanced over his shoulder at her, murder in his eyes.

A moment later the cat-shifter flew through the air, landing in an untidy heap at the bottom of the stairs.

Damon had simply put a hand to the man's chest and shoved, but now he let out his full power with a warning.

"You even *look* at my mate again, and I will reach down your throat, pull out your guts then strangle you with them."

Alastair shifted on the spot. He scrambled out from his suit and left it abandoned as his cat shot forward into the nearest tree to shout insults from its topmost branches.

The executor cleared his throat, then patted his pocket. "Well, I'll leave you all to your private business. We'll take a look at this immediately and get back to you soon as possible."

Niall glared evilly at Damon, but at least he was smart enough to walk away in the opposite direction, avoiding all contact with Addie.

"*You didn't need to scare them that much,*" Abby whispered in his head, amazed they could communicate like that, thrilled she had a mate she could do that with.

Damon showed his teeth. "*Hey, I'm not tracking them down and pulling all the fur from their tails, even though that's what I want to do. See how reasonable I can be?*"

"*Very reasonable. I'm glad.*"

His laughter was clear as they spoke by mind, and joy welled up inside her.

She held out a hand and waited for him to join her, but he motioned instead to someone standing out of her line of sight.

Glenn came forward, hat held in hands. "I never would've believed it, but we have a chance."

"More than a chance," Damon assured him. "I looked the papers over, and while I'm no expert, I think they're real. I hope to hear good news on your behalf soon."

The gardener nodded. "We'll all be forever grateful to you if that happens. Thank you for standing up for us. That takes a good man, and I'm proud to have met you, sir."

Addie stepped forward and linked her hand through

Damon's. A deep sense of longing rolled from him, and she wondered at it.

"Addie, my love. Would you mind living in Scotland for a little longer?"

"What, you're not going to drag me to the bright lights of New York City and make me soak in the decadence?"

"I love you, sweetheart."

He added a little nip to the words, as if a kiss had been pressed to her mind, squeezing her fingers as he turned back to Glenn.

"I have a proposition. If it does turn out you inherit, give me a call. Splitting the castle between the group might be difficult, but if you sell the place, you can all have a share."

Glenn nodded, confusion muddying his eyes. "But part of the idea was to keep my grandmam here."

Damon nodded. "If I buy the manor, you can all stay on. I've never owned a castle before. I imagine it takes a fair bit of work to keep it up."

The gardener flashed a smile.

"Don't get too excited until we find out for sure it's yours," Damon warned, "but here's where you can reach me. For this, or anything else you need."

Addie waited until Glenn had marched off, Damon's business card in his fingers. She shook her head in confusion as she patted his nonexistent pockets. "Where did you get that from, and how can you possibly offer to buy this place?"

Damon cleared his throat. "We still have a bit of talking to do."

Addie snickered—there was nothing else she could do. "It appears we do."

"Would you be upset to discover you're mated to a wealthy man?"

"Only if I were an idiot," she replied. "Come on. You can tell me all about it over lunch."

"Naked lunch?" Damon suggested.

"Talking lunch," Addie insisted.

He hummed in disapproval before brightening, a grin dancing over his expression. "Tell you what, we'll play a game of checkers to decide which we do first—your memory can't help you win *that* game."

She laughed and led her mischievous wolf back into the manor, enjoying the steady stream of happiness and satisfaction rolling off him through their linked fingers.

Happiness, satisfaction and a solid dose of lust. She could handle all of that, with or without cheating at checkers.

EPILOGUE

One year later.

*D*amon caught her, twirling her in the air before pressing her shoulders to the wooden wall of the stable. Addie laughed, the sound turning into a moan of pleasure as he pushed up her skirt and slipped his fingers into her, testing her wetness. "Every damn time. Every damn time you're ready for me."

"Now," she begged. "Hurry, Damon. Someone could come along any moment."

Damon shoved aside his kilt. There was no time for finesse or long foreplay, although they had been fooling around in the hayloft for the past hour, so that totally counted. He lined up his cock and thrust, pinning her to the wall as he protected her with an arm behind her hips and shoulders. Addie tangled her fingers in his hair and pulled as he drove forward, pounding into her.

It was his favourite position, and by now, she knew it. She knew everything about him.

"*You're going to be the death of me,*" he whispered into her mind. "*So damn addicted I can't breathe without you.*"

"You say the sweetest—oh, my God, there. *There.*"

He chuckled, his laughter turning into exploding pleasure as she tightened around him, dragging a climax from him faster than he ever would've thought possible.

Except he should've expected it. This was what his mate did to him.

Even after a year of being together, he couldn't resist the touch of her skin or the taste of her lips. He loved waking up in the morning with her tangled around him, a steady stream of emotion pouring between them as if she'd spent the entire night stroking him. Caring for him.

And when they fought, she held nothing back. She shared it all, and her frustration and fiery darts dashed over him as she let him have it when he'd done something stupid, which tended to be at least every other day.

Makeup sex as mates was like nothing on earth.

He slowly lowered her to the ground, dipping to press a kiss to her cheek. She sighed happily as she straightened his shirt and rearranged his kilt. "Are you still glad we live here?"

"At the manor? Of course. It's the best home I've ever had." He caught her by the chin and nipped her lower lip. "And it's got you, which makes it perfect."

"Hello. Are we in the right place?"

A shout rang from the door, and Addie darted under his arm with a squeal, racing forward to tackle hug a stunning copper-haired woman.

Damon was only a step behind, eager to see his friend Jim again.

They'd visited with Lillie and Jim in the Yukon last

summer, and then again at Christmas. They'd seen each a half dozen times over the past year, but this was the first time it had worked for their friends to make the trip to Scotland.

Lillie and Addie walked ahead of them toward the gardens, arms wrapped around each other like the best friends they would always be.

"You'd think those two hadn't talked in years," Jim grumbled good-naturedly, accepting the cigar Damon offered, "instead of having Skyped less than twelve hours ago."

"Addie's never going to forgive me for taking an entire month to hook up high-speed Internet," Damon said, mock weariness in his voice.

"Ha." Jim poked his cigar at him. "You weren't here for most of that time. I thought that's when you were in New York introducing her to the family and all the wolf clans you had to impress."

"Hey, it wasn't my idea to take over leadership of Scotland."

It had been the weirdest thing ever, having a supremely regal grey-haired Alpha wolf show up on their doorstep one day and simply offer him leadership without any bloodshed.

Well, okay, it hadn't been *quite* as simple as that, but close.

"Never thought you'd settle down," Jim admitted.

Damon looked over the gardens and the crew of people working for them to keep the manor running. Glenn caught him watching and dipped his head, slipping into position to unobtrusively guard the ladies as they headed into the labyrinth.

Damon was no longer a lone wolf. He'd found his mate, and in the months that followed, he'd found people to care for. People who cared for him and Addie. Their pack was exactly what Addie had predicted. Lone wolves, foxes, solitary bears, and a few Highland Tigers, although most definitely *not* the Sterling-Wyldes.

They sat on one of the balconies later that night, Grandmam Susanna's delicious dinner settling in their stomachs, Addie curled up in his lap.

A vintage bottle of whisky sat beside his elbow ready to be shared with their friends when they joined them in a few minutes.

"Did you ever think this is the turn your life would take?" Addie whispered against his cheek, her love an eternal kiss against his heart.

"Never." And yet...

Below them on the wide expanse of lawn, a wolf shifter charged, rolling into a bear who'd just emerging from the trees, knocking the big creature to the ground. Damon laughed softly, thinking of his friendship with Jim. How it had seemed so out of place to many people, but turned out so right.

"Never, and yet this is right where I belong." He tilted her head back and stared into her big beautiful eyes. "With you. My mate."

Our mate, his wolf insisted.

Addie laughed.

~

New York Times Bestselling Author Vivian Arend
brings you a series of light-hearted,
stand-alone novellas filled with shifters of all kinds—bears,
wolves, lynx. Whether they're fated mates or falling head-
over-paws, there's always a happily-ever-after.

~

Takhini Shifters
Copper King
Laird Wolf
A Lady's Heart
Wild Prince

~

ABOUT THE AUTHOR

New York Times and *USA Today* bestselling author Vivian Arend loves to share the products of her over-active imagination with her readers. She writes contemporary, western, and light-hearted paranormal romances. The stories are humorous yet emotional, usually with a large cast of family or friends, and a guaranteed happily-ever-after.

Vivian lives in British Columbia, Canada, with her husband of many years—her inspiration for every hero and a willing companion for all sorts of adventures.

Find out more at www.vivianarend.com.